CHERRY LOVER

Cherry #2

VICTORIA QUINN

Hartwick Publishing

Cherry Lover

Contents

1. Slate	1
2. Monroe	23
3. Slate	41
4. Monroe	49
5. Slate	59
6. Monroe	85
7. Slate	91
8. Monroe	103
9. Slate	113
10. Monroe	129
11. Slate	133
12. Monroe	145
13. Slate	153
14. Monroe	167
15. Slate	171
16. Monroe	175
17. Slate	181
18. Monroe	185
19. Slate	195
20. Monroe	201
21. Slate	205
Epilogue	211
From Hartwick Publishing	217
The Banker - Chapter 1	219
The Banker - Chapter 2	225
The Banker - Chapter 3	235

1

Slate

THE OFFICE WAS A PARADISE WHILE COEN AND SIMONE were away. They spent a week in the Bahamas, somewhere remote where he didn't even have an internet connection most of the time. That prevented him from flooding my email with updates.

It was nice.

I tried to enjoy the calm before he returned—with the devil on his arm.

I wondered how long she would play nice before she showed her true colors. Would she stick around for at least a year just to make it seem like their marriage was real? Or would she waste no time and get rid of him in just a few weeks?

The sooner, the better in my opinion. Once the truth was out, Coen would know I had his best interests at heart—and I tried to warn him.

Max walked into my office a moment later, his folder tucked under his arm. "Haven't heard from you in a while."

"You can just call."

"Yes, but you need pictures. I'm not sending that over

email." He set the folder on my desk. "The line of eager girls just keeps getting bigger and bigger. What's the holdup?"

A single woman was the holdup. "We're going to have to put this operation on hold for three months."

"Three months?" he asked blankly. "Why? You keep putting this on hold over and over. What's the problem?"

I paid him, so I got to be the one to ask questions—not the other way around. "It doesn't matter. But I'm not taking new clients for the foreseeable future."

"Does that mean you have one client in mind?"

I was sleeping with the same woman over and over again, a woman so vanilla, but she tasted so sweet. "Yes." The last woman I had committed to was Simone, and that ended up being a mistake. I didn't consider myself to be committed to Monroe in the same way, but I was definitely monogamous.

"So is this just three months?" he asked. "Or do you think it may be indefinite…"

It couldn't be indefinite. I didn't want to lose Monroe, but I didn't want to marry her either.

"Because I need to find a new client if you're retiring."

"I'm not retiring. I'll keep paying you."

"Until you decide in three months?"

There was no decision. This thing I had with Monroe couldn't last forever. Hopefully, I would grow tired of her in three months—and then I could let her go without regret. Maybe she was just a drug I needed in my system until it started to poison me. Or maybe it was going to turn me into an addict. "I'll let you know in three months, Max."

———

I WAS at my place when she called me.

"Hey, sweetheart." I sipped my scotch as I stood at the window and looked at the city. Now that fall had officially arrived, the colors of Central Park were beginning to change.

The leaves were once deep green and vibrant, and now they were showcased tones of yellow and red.

"Don't sweetheart me," she hissed.

I smiled, knowing she had figured out what I'd done. "I wish I could see your face right now. You look so cute when you're mad."

"Trust me, I don't look cute right now."

"I doubt that."

She growled into the phone, but even that sounded cute. "I told you I didn't want your money yet."

"And I didn't give it to you."

"But you went behind my back and paid off my loan."

"I didn't go behind your back. And you're welcome, by the way."

"That's my financial business," she countered. "So yes, you did go behind my back."

I knew she wouldn't take my money up front, so I took matters into my own hands. "I just saved you six thousand dollars over the next three months."

"But that wasn't the deal."

"What's the problem?" I asked. "Were you planning on leaving before the three months are up?" I drank from my glass again and let the ice cube touch my lips.

"I'd like the option…"

The idea of her wanting to leave didn't please me. I thought we were both in this for the next three months, to see if it went anywhere, if it *could* go anywhere. "And why would you like the option?"

"Just in case my heart starts to get crushed."

I would never hurt her—at least, not on purpose. "Well, now you have to see it through." I'd successfully caged her, made her a prisoner without her consent. She couldn't pay back the money because it'd been given directly to the bank. Now she had to earn her freedom.

"That worked out for you."

"And it helped your motivation."

She turned quiet, still angry with me but not angry enough to hang up the phone.

"How was your day?" I asked, trying to change the subject.

"I'm not in the mood for chitchat."

"Just in the mood to yell at me?" I teased.

"Yes. Now that I've done that…I'm gonna go." She hung up without saying goodbye.

I didn't call her back, and I finished the liquor in my glass. Maybe paying back her medical bill without her consent was unethical, but I didn't care. It would save her a lot of money over the next three months, and for someone like her, that money made all the difference in the world. If she really walked away from me, I wouldn't stop her. She had more power than she realized.

———

I SHOWED up on her doorstep an hour later.

She opened the door, looking both sexy and pissed. "I'm surprised you didn't just let yourself inside."

"I was tempted."

She shut the door in my face.

I slipped my foot in the crack so the door wouldn't close. I invited myself inside, seeing the TV playing an old rerun of *Friends*, while the blanket was rumpled on the sofa from where she'd been lying.

"Please come in…" She moved into the kitchen and pulled out a bottle of wine.

I wasn't a fan of her apartment. It was on the bad side of town, and the walls were so thin I could hear everything her neighbors did. Sometimes I was afraid a man would realize a beautiful woman lived here alone and try to do something sinister. When I encouraged her to move closer to the center of Manhattan, she said she could never afford it, even without all those loans to pay. She would rather save her money to buy something someday.

Maybe I should just buy her something.

Man, that would really piss her off.

She returned with two glasses of wine. "Here."

"Thanks." I'd just finished a glass of scotch before I came over here, so the wine wasn't a good chaser. But I brought it to my lips and took a drink anyway. I stared at her as I felt the red wine across my tongue, a cheap five-dollar wine she must have picked up at the bodega on the corner. I didn't mean to judge her for the thrifty items she bought, but I was used to the finer things in life.

Her neighbor started to scream at his wife, yelling obscenities that would make anyone call the police.

But she didn't flinch at the sound.

"Do you think we should call someone?" I asked.

"I've already tried. I've called the police several times, but nothing ever changes. They take him to jail, he's there for a week or so, and then he gets out and comes back to the apartment. They fight again, and the process repeats itself."

"If he's beating her, he could go to jail for a long time."

"I have a feeling she's not pressing charges. She's probably too scared of his retaliation."

That seemed to be the main problem with domestic abuse. There was no real solution. Once the man got out of jail, he would be so pissed off that he might kill her this time. "Then maybe you should relocate. Find an apartment closer to work."

"Like I said, I can't afford it."

"But you *can* afford it." Her rent would be twice as expensive, but at least she would be safe every night. Now I didn't know if I wanted to leave her here every night when she didn't stay at my place, especially when she came home from work in those cute outfits.

"I shouldn't spend most of my check on rent. Now I can afford groceries again. I still need health insurance, haircuts, and all those other fundamentals."

"But wouldn't you rather spend a little more to be in a safe place?"

Instead of drinking her wine, she gave me a ferocious look. "I know I don't live in a palace, but that doesn't make you better than me. This is all I can afford, and I'm okay with that. I'm grateful I have a roof over my head and food on the table."

"Wait, you don't have health insurance?"

She shook her head.

"How can you not have health insurance? Isn't that provided at your job?"

"There's a small benefits package, but it really doesn't cover much."

"I just don't think this part of town is safe."

"It's New York," she said. "It's one of the most dangerous places to live. It doesn't matter where you go."

No, it did matter. "You know it's the law. You're supposed to have health insurance."

She rolled her eyes. "When you're as broke as I am, you aren't afraid to break the law. It wasn't until last month that I even had enough cash to cover a single payment. So back off a little."

How could I back off when I was unhappy with all of her decisions?

She finished her wine and set the empty glass on the entryway table. "So, you pissed me off by paying back my debt, and now you're here to patronize me? I assumed you came here to get laid."

"I did."

"Well, you aren't getting me in the mood, that's for sure."

Where she lived and her health insurance shouldn't be my concern if I only wanted to fuck her. She wasn't my girlfriend, so her safety wasn't my priority. I shouldn't care at all, but anytime I was in her apartment, I wanted to make her life better. I wanted to shower her with beautiful things so she would never have to worry about making rent or getting food on the table. All that stuff would be taken care of.

Now the weather had turned milder, she wore skintight denim jeans with holes in the knees and heeled olive booties. She wore a black t-shirt that hugged her curves nicely while her brown cardigan hung by the door. Whether she was in a dress or covered head to toe, she looked stunning. For not having any money, she knew how to shop on a budget. She walked up to me and took the glass out of my hands, even though I'd had barely a sip. "If you're done berating me, you should go." She gathered both of the glasses and placed them in the kitchen sink.

Voicing my concerns only seemed to annoy her, and it appeared she wouldn't take my recommendations anyway. Perhaps the world was simpler to me because I had the money to make my problems go away. Monroe didn't have that luxury, despite the fact that I had erased all of her debts. She still had an average salary, and in a place as expensive as New York, that salary made the working-class poor—especially as a one-income person. If she had a man to split the bills with, her social standing would be much different.

But I got in the way of that. She could have kept dating Wyatt and that may have gone somewhere, but I got rid of him so I could enjoy her myself, even though I had nothing long term to offer her.

She stared at me as she waited for me to walk out the door.

I wasn't going anywhere. "I'm too tired to go home now. I'll crash here."

"In my crummy apartment?" she asked incredulously.

"I never said your apartment was crummy. I just don't like your neighbors."

"Well, I'm making peanut butter and jelly sandwiches for dinner."

I shrugged. "Then that's what we'll have." I walked into her bedroom and stripped off my t-shirt. Her bed was just two mattresses piled on top of a steel frame. There wasn't a headboard. One dresser was against the wall, but it looked old, like she'd picked it up from a flea market. When I was down to my boxers, I lay on the bed, feeling the slight discomfort in my lower back because the mattress was clearly old.

She stepped into the doorway and leaned against the frame. "You have no problem making yourself at home, huh?"

"Not really." I interlocked my fingers behind my head and stared at her, hoping those clothes would start dropping to the floor.

"Some might say that's rude."

"And others might say you're in my debt—and I can do whatever I want."

Her eyes narrowed at my assholish comment. "I might owe you my time, but you certainly don't own me."

"I disagree." I got off the bed and slowly walked toward her, enticed by this cat-and-mouse game. Her resistance was genuine rather than part of a dirty game, but that made it even better. I stopped in front of her, watching her keep her steady gaze as she looked into mine.

Her breathing slowly increased as she remained the recipient of my gaze. She kept the fire in her eyes, but the rest of her body was wavering. She was either intimidated or aroused by the way I swallowed her whole.

"Take off your clothes." My eyes moved down her neck to the t-shirt she wore, the thin fabric that separated my eyes from her beautiful flesh. "Now." I'd paid a lot of money to own this woman, and I intended to cash in every single penny in return. She didn't have the power to tell me no, not for the next three months. So I knew how I wanted to fuck her. I wanted her on her hands and knees, ass in my face, with my big dick sliding through that small pussy.

She still resisted me in silence but eventually snapped under the weight of my intimidation. She slowly peeled off her top then unhooked her bra in the back. It fell to the floor and revealed her perfect tits, busty boobs with perfect nipples. She studied the way I stared at her, the way my eyes devoured her tits.

"The rest."

She popped the button on her jeans and pulled those down, leaving the boots for last. She unzipped them then peeled off her socks. Once her shoes were gone, she was two inches shorter.

I rested my arm against the wall and leaned in as I examined her, cherishing the feminine curves that made her devastatingly beautiful. She had an hourglass figure, tight thighs that I loved to kiss before I kissed her pussy, and a sexy belly button. Her fair skin was as white as the clouds and soft like a rose petal. Everything about her was perfect, like she wasn't even real. A surgeon had made all of her features ideal, had turned her from an ordinary woman into an extraordinary one. Why did she work in the marketing department when she should be the face of her clothing line? "I've been with a lot of women in my life…none of them compare to you." I dragged the backs of my fingers down her neck then over her collarbone. She was like a doll I liked to play with, always careful with her because she might break. My hand moved to her cheek, and I saw the way she turned into the touch.

I was hard in my boxers, so thick and ready that the thin material could barely contain me. A wet spot had soiled the front of the fabric, a sign of arousal I wouldn't want to hide even if I could. My hand pushed my boxers down so my cock could appear, long and throbbing for the woman in front of me.

She glanced at him before she looked me in the eye again.

My hands cupped both of her tits, and I massaged them hard, caressing them intimately in my hands. My fingers tested the firmness, and my thumbs flicked over her hard nipples. I'd been obsessed with all of her since the moment I laid eyes on her, but her tits, in particular, were exquisite. She had such a petite rib cage with such a busty chest. The lack of proportion made her more desirable. "I love your tits." I flattened her against the wall as my hands continued to grip her anxiously. "I'll tit-fuck them eventually." I would love to slide my big cock through those lubed boobs. I would love to come all over her face and neck, to remind her who owned her.

My boxers slid to the floor, and I pressed farther up against her, my lips so close I could almost touch hers. My cock pressed into her stomach, and the precome oozing from my tip smeared against her warm skin. My hands kept groping her tits, feeling her pulse under her skin. I felt her chest rise and fall as her breathing quickened, as the arousal erased all the rage she felt toward me.

"Have you ever been tit-fucked, sweetheart?" It seemed like all she'd ever done was give a blow job. The boys before me weren't man enough to go down on her, to treasure these perfect tits in their big hands. She was so inexperienced, and that turned me on like crazy. I'd already popped her cherry, but everything else was just as enjoyable.

"No."

I squeezed both of her tits as I leaned in and kissed her. I gave her a searing-hot kiss, a warning of what I wanted to do with her once I got her on the bed. I loved watching her underneath me, her tits shaking and her eyes filled with tears. But now I wanted to fuck her in a new way, on her hands and knees with her ass in my face. I wanted to stare at her asshole as I pushed my dick deep inside her.

As our kiss escalated, she arched her back and pressed her tits farther into my hands. Her fingers wrapped around my length, and she jerked me off slightly, spreading the lubrication from my tip down to my base. There was enough of it that she could easily glide her hand up and down, squeezing my length with the perfect pressure.

She was so inexperienced but so talented at the same time.

I gripped her waist and guided her to the bed. "On your hands and knees."

She crawled onto the bed then looked at me over her shoulder, her cunt gleaming with her slickness.

I didn't bring lube with me, so hopefully that pussy was wet enough to make this happen. I'd fucked her enough times that she should be stretched out, but she still usually produced a few tears when I was inside her. I'd never heard of a woman taking this long to break in, but I was enjoying it. Once she finally acclimated to my size, she would never want another man. Any other dick would be much too small in comparison. She would never be satisfied.

I licked my palm and spread it over the head of my cock so I would have slick entrance. "Open your legs wider."

She stretched her knees apart on the bed.

"Arch your back."

She pressed her stomach toward the mattress and lifted her ass to the sky.

"Perfect." I wrapped her hair around my fist before I gripped the back of her neck. Then I pressed the head of my cock slowly into her opening, feeling the moisture surround me the instant I was inside. "Fuck..." It didn't matter how many times I fucked her. I could never get used to how incredible she felt. She had the most amazing pussy in the world. I slowly pushed farther into her, trying to get all the way inside that tight channel.

She resisted me like always, probably because she didn't have any lube this time. She breathed harder as she felt me deeper, felt me stretch her wide apart. No matter how many times I took her, she would probably never be able to take me in a single thrust. She simply wasn't anatomically inclined to do it.

I pushed farther inside, listening to the way she breathed in response.

She started to moan, either from pleasure or pain.

I kept going until most of my length was deep inside. I could feel her walls cling to me tightly because I was such an intrusion. Her wetness surrounded me, but it might not be enough to keep our bodies gliding together.

My eyes moved to her little asshole, the little gem I hadn't had the chance to meet. I intended to fuck her there, but if her pussy could barely handle my length, her asshole would be an even tighter fit. "I'm going to fuck you harder this time." I gave a slight tug on her hair and made her chin tilt toward the ceiling. "If you ask me to slow down, I won't listen." She sold herself to me, so I got to fulfill all of my fantasies. I sucked my thumb for several seconds before I pressed it against her asshole.

She immediately jerked at the intrusion, releasing a moan and a grunt. "What are you doing?"

I yanked on her hair again. "Whatever I want." I pressed my thumb harder into her, pressing against her bottom wall so I could feel the outline of my dick in her pussy. Then I started to thrust, smacking into her so her ass shook slightly.

She released a loud moan at my first thrust, like she wasn't prepared for the anaconda that slammed into her.

I'd been fucking her slow and easy for a long time, and now I just wanted to fuck her how I wanted. I'd given her pussy enough time to get used to me, and if it didn't want to cooperate, I would make it. I fucked her good and hard, slamming my dick deep inside her as I felt her arousal act as a lubricant. Her asshole tightened around my finger every time I hit her deep. When I pulled out, it relaxed, only to tighten again when I thrust once more. I could fuck her deeper at this angle, so I knew she was taking more of me than usual.

Then she started to cry.

Biggest fucking turn-on of all.

I gripped her neck tighter and fucked her harder as I listened to her cry. The sound of her sniffles and watery moan only made my dick thicken. I didn't enjoy hurting a woman, but I did when her discomfort was caused by the size of my dick.

That's why I loved fucking virgins so much.

Their pain turned me on as much as their pleasure.

My hand released her hair and gripped her shoulder, getting a better hold on the woman taking my dick. I pulled back slightly, making her arch her back and stick out her ass a little more.

I scooted a little closer and lost myself completely, fucking her like a man who'd just paid for a whore. I grunted as I tore that pussy apart, falling into the pleasure that radiated from my spine to every limb.

The only reason I stopped was because I hadn't made her come.

I would be an asshole if I didn't.

I moved my hand between her legs and rubbed her clit as I slowed down my thrusts. My cock was ready to blow, so slowing down was the best move anyway. It took a lot of vigorous rubbing to get her where I wanted her to be, and once she was at the edge of the cliff, she fell.

Her hips bucked into my hand, and she moaned as she came, my dick shoved deep inside her cunt. She arched her back deeper then bounced back against my dick, wanting more thrusts as she finished.

I waited until she was completely done before I slammed into her again, fucking her as aggressively as I had earlier. I was already rock-hard and on the threshold, so it only took a few pumps for me to have an incredible orgasm, an explosion that made me grunt. "Fuck…" I stared at her asshole as my ass tightened and my dick twitched. I pumped all my come inside her, giving it to her as deep as possible. The sensation was so exquisite, the best orgasm I'd ever had.

But I said that every time I fucked her.

I let my cock soften before I pulled out of her, the come seeping out of her entrance right away. There was so much that her tiny cunt couldn't contain it all. The area around her lips was a little red from the thick crown of my cock as it pushed inside her.

Monroe got off the bed right away and walked into the bathroom.

I lay on the bed and looked at the window, which was covered by the closed blinds. A second later, I heard the shower run. I didn't want her to rinse off because I wanted her to be full of my come for as long as possible. I also thought it was weird that she was in the shower, considering she never showered at night.

I decided to join her.

Her bathroom was smaller than my closet, so squeezing inside was a little more difficult than usual. At least it brought us close together under the warm water.

Her makeup was gone because she'd already washed it off under the warm water. Now she was purposely not looking at me, her hair pulled up into a bun so it wouldn't get wet. It didn't seem like she needed a shower at all, but instead wanted to get away from me.

"What's wrong?" I asked, having no idea what I did to upset her. We were fine just minutes ago when she was coming against my fingers. Her pussy had tightened around me as she was taken to a spiritual place.

She caught the water in her palms before she splashed it onto her face. "Nothing."

"Why do I feel like you're lying?"

Her eyes were directed elsewhere. "Because I am."

My hand moved under her chin, and I forced her gaze to rise. "Sweetheart, what is it?"

"That, right there." She pushed my hand down. "You can't call me sweetheart after you treat me like that."

"Treat you like what?"

"Screwing me like that...telling me you won't slow down...fucking me like I'm a toy rather than a person." The water hit her beautiful skin then dripped to the drain. Her nipples weren't hard anymore, and her skin was a little paler than it had been minutes ago. Even though she bathed in warm water, she seemed cold as ice.

"I know you're inexperienced, but that's how people fuck."

"While the woman cries?" she asked incredulously.

"You always cry. You've cried every single time I've fucked you."

"Because it hurts, asshole. Why do you like it so much? What's wrong with you? You like hurting me?"

For a brief moment, I felt like an asshole for getting off to her discomfort, but then that guilt disappeared an instant later. "I told you that's what I like. I won't apologize for it. And I particularly enjoy it when you cry. I've never fucked a virgin more than once, but I doubt they cry every time afterward. You're particularly small—"

"You're too big. I'm not the problem. You are."

My length was unusual, I would give her that. "I went easy on you the first few times. You can't expect me to do that forever."

"If you want to call me sweetheart, yes, I do." She crossed her arms over her chest. "I understand this is just a fantasy to you. I understand you paid me to get what you want. But I thought you would be good to me, go easy on me until I'm up to your speed. I thought this would be more of a partnership. I feel like...a whore or something." She shifted her gaze away from mine, like she could barely say the truth out loud.

That was exactly how I felt as I fucked her. I let the water soak into my hair and drip down my muscular physique as I considered what response to give. I should tell her that her feelings didn't matter, that she would do whatever I wanted because that was our arrangement. But I saw this woman as more than just someone I liked to fuck. I saw her as my friend...as someone I cared about. "Alright."

"Alright what?" She turned back to me.

"I won't apologize for what happened because I warned you about my character. But I'll break you in first...nice and slow. When you're ready, I want to fuck you the way I want. It'll be hard, it'll be deep. Sometimes it'll be in your pussy. Sometimes your mouth. And sometimes your ass."

———

I SAT on the couch with my feet firmly planted against the rug. My hands gripped the soft skin of her hips, feeling her rise and fall on my length at her own pace. I relaxed against the cushion and watched her move up and down, push my dick past her pussy lips and take me deep inside her.

Now I was focused on stretching out that pussy, molding her to my size so she could enjoy me without being over-whelmed by pain. I stopped rocking my hips up and hitting her from below, letting her pick the pace. It was hard for me to sit back and do nothing, but it felt so good to have her cunt sheathe me over and over.

We'd been doing this for the last twenty minutes, and she still hadn't dried up. Somehow, her phenomenal pussy could keep us wet enough to continue on. I never thought slow sex could be so enjoyable, but vanilla had become my new favorite flavor.

I grabbed her hips and stationed her on my dick, keeping her on my lap as I took a deep breath and came inside her. I moaned as I looked at her phenomenal tits, giving her a load of come that turned me on all over again. Once I was completely finished, I grabbed her hips and started to move her again. "Keep going." That climax was satisfying, but I was still so aroused that I stayed hard. I guided her up and down, pushing through my come as I slid back inside her pussy. She was still insanely tight, so I would have to fuck her dozens of times before she finally easily accepted my girth.

She dug her hands into my hair and leaned into me, her tits pressed against my chest. "I like this…"

My lips moved against hers as I spoke. "Me too." Knowing she enjoyed it turned me on, just the way her tears turned me on. All I had to do was sit here and watch this beautiful woman fuck me with a pussy that constantly stayed wet. I squeezed her ass cheeks and breathed against her mouth, my dick so wet that it never wanted to leave. I could just keep coming and coming…

Her lips trembled against mine as she came, her nails clawing at my shoulders while her pussy constricted around me. "God…" She panted hard and ground her clit against my body as she finished, her hips bucking automatically.

I pressed my fingers against her clit and rubbed hard, wanting her to finish with endless waves of pleasure. I felt all the slickness across my fingers, all the arousal she felt because of me. There were no tears in her eyes this time, probably because she was taking it so slow. When she finished, I pulled my fingers away and gripped her tits, fondling them as I felt our come mix together.

"I shouldn't have waited so long…" She pressed her palms against my chest.

I was the only man to have fucked this beautiful woman, and that turned me on like crazy. "Yes, you should have. Because this pussy is mine." It was perfectly tight, perfectly wet, and perfectly perfect. I'd never fucked a better cunt.

She continued to rise up and down, rocking her hips as she moved with me, her hands holding on to me like an anchor.

The intercom beeped, and my mother's voice filled the

room. "Honey, it's your mother. I was in the neighborhood and wanted to stop by."

I growled as the sensual moment was shattered. I'd already come twice, but I could have gone a third time. But the sound of my mother's voice instantly zapped all the arousal from my body.

The same thing happened to her. "Your mother is coming over?"

"Trust me, I had no idea."

She got off my lap and then snatched her clothes off the ground. "I guess I'll hide in your room."

"You don't have to hide." I pulled on my boxers and sweatpants. "But you do have to put some clothes on."

She walked down the hallway to get dressed.

I pressed the intercom. "Come on up, Mother." I hit the button so the elevator would rise.

When I turned around, I spotted Monroe's black thong on the ground right next to the couch. I quickly kicked it under the couch just as the doors opened to reveal my mother, dressed in black slacks, a teal blouse, and an expensive coat.

"Hey, honey. Hope I'm not intruding by stopping by."

"Not at all, Mother." I kissed her on the cheek then quickly pulled away, afraid that I smelled like sex and perfume. "What brings you here?" I walked to the kitchen and opened a bottle of wine and poured two glasses.

"I was visiting Carol. She lives on the tenth floor."

"And how did that go?" I came back to her and handed her a glass.

"Very well." She accepted the glass and took a drink, her red lipstick smearing across the rim. "We played bridge."

"Sounds exciting."

"Not really. I'm much better at bridge than she is." She helped herself to the couch in the living room. "So I spoke to your brother today. It sounds like he and Simone are having a great time in the Bahamas."

"Hope he can enjoy it while it lasts." I sat in the leather armchair across from her, not uncomfortable in my bare skin and sweatpants. This was how I dressed whenever I relaxed at home, so I refused to change just because she was there—especially when she gave me no warning.

"Stop it. Simone might have a change of heart. You never know."

I laughed into my glass. "That bitch won't change her mind. All she cares about is power and money. That will never change."

"I hope you're wrong. Because your brother seems very happy…"

He watched Simone walk down the aisle like she was a dream come true. It was sad, like watching a deer about to be shot by a hunter five hundred feet away. "I wish I was wrong too. But I'm not." My brother had made the worst mistake of his life, and once the dust settled, he would have to live with the humiliation of his stupidity.

Footsteps sounded, and Monroe emerged from the hallway, dressed in the jeans and long-sleeved shirt she'd arrived in. "Hello, Elizabeth." Her hair had been combed, and she presented herself like she hadn't been fucked for the last thirty minutes, like there weren't two loads of come sitting inside her that very moment.

My mother beamed once she entered the room. "Monroe, what a nice surprise." She rose to her feet and gave Monroe a kiss on the cheek. "I hope I didn't interrupt your evening. I didn't realize you were here."

"She's here often, Mother." I didn't want to be rude, but she should give me a heads-up when she was stopping by. We both probably smelled like sex if you got too close to us.

"Good. I hope that means I'll be seeing a lot of you, then." Mother sat down again and picked up her glass.

Monroe sat beside me and helped herself to the glass of wine I'd poured for myself. "So you're a good bridge player?"

"One of the best," my mom said proudly. "My sister taught me."

"I've never played."

"You're too young to know how to play, but I could always teach you."

"Sure," Monroe said.

"You've never offered to teach me," I pointed out.

"Because you only care about poker and cigars," my mother jabbed. "After I teach Monroe, maybe she can teach you."

It seemed like my mother had a new favorite.

"You smoke cigars?" Monroe asked me.

"Yes." I ignored the disapproval in her voice. "Occasionally."

"Well, occasionally is going to turn into never," Monroe said.

Mother smiled. "I like her even more now."

"I should have known the two of you would gang up on me," I said with a sigh. "It's ironic because you should be ganging up on Simone."

"I believe in karma," Mother said. "Simone will get what's coming to her."

"Like how she betrayed me and then got my brother to stab me in the back?" I countered. "How she cheated on me and lied to me, but she's still getting what she wants? Karma is a bunch of bullshit."

Mother watched me for a long time, and instead of looking at me with sympathy, she looked at me with disappointment. "I didn't realize you were so bitter about it. Bitter isn't good for anyone, son. It'll sit inside your soul, make its way to your heart, and eventually kill you. Let the past stay in the past."

People kept telling me that, but they were unsympathetic.

"That would be easy to do if I didn't have to see them together every day, if I didn't have to watch my own brother betray me. Being bitter is better than being a pussy. I won't look the other way and pretend it's water under the bridge, not when I've never gotten an apology. I won't look the other way while my brother makes the biggest mistake of his life. You say I'm the one who needs to let it go—but you're the one who let go too soon."

2

Monroe

THE BED SWALLOWED MY SMALL FRAME AS I SANK INTO THE mattress, the weight of this large man pushing me deeper into the sheets. His sweat filled the space between us with more heat, making the temperature increase many degrees so the cool sheets were warm with body heat. I lay there as he overtook me, his narrow hips between my thighs and his powerful arms pinned beneath my legs.

It'd gotten easier take him over the past week, but every single time, it was gentle and slow. He treated me with perfect gentleness, like every time was my first time. My nails slid across the slickness of his back so they could never really pierce the skin. I gave him a few scratches here and there, but nothing that would leave permanent marks.

We didn't need to use lube anymore, which meant it was getting more comfortable for me to take him.

He kept his eyes locked on me as he watched the emotions dance across my face. He wore that sexy expression, with his jaw tight and his eyes narrowed. He'd shaved that morning, but the shadow was already coming back, giving him that darker look I loved. "I need you to come, sweetheart."

I already did once, but he wanted me to finish so he could

finally let go. I'd been on the verge anyway, so it didn't take that long. His cock was hitting the magic button deep inside me, igniting my senses and bringing me to life. My fingers latched on to his scalp, and I tightened around him, coating him with my downpour of arousal. My body stiffened before it bucked involuntarily, the bumps rising all over my skin. It felt so good that my thighs squeezed and bruised his hips, and deep moans left my lips.

He watched me for a few seconds before he released, coming inside me with a moan that matched mine, just in deeper shades of masculinity. His heavy come filled me, warm with gravity. His cock always got so big just as he came, thickening noticeably. He gave his final thrust as he finished, his sweaty chest wiping against my tits. He buried his face into my neck as he slowly rocked into me, sliding through our mutual arousal. Heavy and deep, his breathing showed his satisfaction as well as his exhaustion.

I knew he had specific tastes when it came to sex and I didn't fulfill those fantasies, but I loved sex like this, slow and gentle with our eyes connected. I liked it when he used his cock gently to make me feel good rather than hurt me. Maybe it was boring to him, but it certainly wasn't boring to me. I liked kissing him, feeling his heartbeat through his powerful muscles. He'd fucked me hard before and I came, but I didn't feel good all over like I did when we were like this.

Once he caught his breath, he slowly pulled out of me before he rolled over and got comfortable beside me. His king-size bed sat in his dark room, the city lights casting some illumination over the space. He had shutters that rolled down to keep the lights out, but I'd never seen him use them. He lay there in silence as he relaxed, as the sweat evaporated from his chest or soaked into the sheets.

Not only was the sex great, but it sapped my energy almost instantly. I was always ready to go to sleep once the pleasure had seeped into my blood. Like a drug, it knocked me out cold.

Slate's voice caught my attention. "It doesn't seem like you're sore anymore."

"Not really. I've been doing much better." I stuck to my side of the bed because we were both hot.

"Haven't had to use lube."

"Yes, you accomplished the impossible. You stretched me out."

"Took long enough…"

"I'm very petite."

"Yes, I know that better than anyone."

Once I cooled off, I pulled the sheets to my shoulders and got comfortable against the pillow. "Can I sleep here?"

He looked at the ceiling, the strength of his masculine jawline visible even in the shadows. "Yes. Always."

"Be careful what you wish for…this is a very comfy bed." Much better than the moth-eaten cot at my place. I couldn't imagine bringing a date back to screw on that thing. Wasn't exactly sexy.

"I thought you liked it because of the guy."

"Not exactly. I like the guy for fucking me. But now I just want his bed."

He chuckled. "At least you still have some use for me."

"You protect me too. No one can bother me here."

"Do people usually bother you?" He turned his head my way to see my expression.

When I entered my apartment building, I always got a few catcalls from neighbors. That got old, especially since it'd been happening since I first moved in. I'd stopped using the laundry facilities there and just carried it to a place across the street, but I never told him any of that. Here, it was impossible for anyone to ever bother me, and if they were stupid enough to try, I had a six-foot powerhouse to snap their neck.

"No. I just mean I feel really alone here. It's so quiet that it doesn't feel like we're in the city at all."

"That's why I had to have the top floor. I didn't want to hear the traffic on the street. Occasionally, I'll hear a helicopter, but helicopters are cool so that's fine."

"They are cool."

Now that he'd cooled off, he cuddled into my side and rested his face in the crook of my neck. His heavy arm rested across my stomach, bringing new warmth into the sheets. Once fall hit New York, the temperature dropped quickly, and the hot, sticky humidity of summer was just a memory. "Does that mean we can take it up a notch?" he asked, revisiting the main topic that brought us together in the first place.

I had the power in the situation because I could say no, give myself another week to enjoy the slow sex I liked so much. The carnal fucking that he enjoyed, with a hint of his controlling nature, made for hard sex I didn't exactly enjoy. But he'd paid me for a service, and I felt like it would be wrong not to give him what he wanted—especially now that I could handle it. "I think so."

He breathed a deep sigh of pleasure. "Good."

"But can we make a compromise?"

"What kind of compromise?"

"Maybe we could do it slow like that a few times a week…"

He lifted his face so he could look at me. "Now that you're stretched out, you'll like it hard. We rushed into it too fast in the beginning, but it doesn't always hurt like that."

"Maybe. But I like it like this. I like it when it's slow, sensual…"

"You prefer lovemaking rather than fucking?"

I wasn't going to put it in those terms until he did. "I guess…"

"We both know I'm not the lovemaking kind of guy. I made an exception for you."

"And maybe you'll make an exception again…?" I rubbed my hand up his chest, trying to entice him with my affection. "I know you like it."

"I like *you*."

"Then have me like that…once in a while."

His eyes bored into mine as he considered my request for a long time. He finally gave an answer. "A few times a week is too much. Once a week."

That wasn't what I hoped for, but I should be grateful that he compromised with me at all. He was a hard man who liked to call all the shots, so the fact that he was letting me get my way at all was surprising. "Alright. You have a deal."

He cuddled into my side once again and rested his lips against my hairline. "Good."

He squeezed me to his chest then sighed, as if he was about to fall asleep. "Night, Cherry."

I had just closed my eyes, but now I opened them again at the nickname. "Cherry?"

"I'm sure you understand the significance."

"Yes, but it's not very cute."

"How so?"

"You've popped hundreds of other women's cherries. That doesn't make me special."

"That's where you're wrong. All I ever do is make compromises with you. All I do is try to make you stay. You're the only woman I can't stop wanting. You're the most expensive cherry I've ever bought. I don't know what it means…but it means something."

———

I DID the walk of shame back to my apartment early in the morning. His car dropped me off at the curb, and I made my way inside. The mornings were always the worst because it was so cool outside. Fall had just begun, but there a chill in the air right when the sun came out.

I walked to my apartment but stopped when I noticed the door was cracked.

I would never leave the door open like that.

I listened for a moment, wondering if the super was inside my apartment or maybe someone who wasn't supposed to be there. I tapped my knuckles on the door and spoke into the empty living room. "You done yet?"

No answer.

I pushed the door opened and peered inside.

The living room was empty.

Everything had been taken. My TV was gone, the entertainment stand it stood on was missing, and my couch left a line of dust on the floor where it'd been. They took my entryway table. The only thing on the floor was a photograph of my mother and me.

At least they left that behind.

I went into the kitchen and saw all my appliances had disappeared. Even the fridge was missing. "How the hell did they steal a fridge?" I opened the cabinets and saw all my glasses had vanished. My silverware was gone.

They basically took every single possession I had.

"Oh no...not my clothes." I ran into my bedroom and wasn't surprised to see my bed and nightstands had been taken, along with my small dresser. But when I opened my closet door, I was truly heartbroken.

They took everything.

All my bargain outfits I had hunted for at the discount stores. I waited until designer stuff was basically donated two years after it went out of style and waited until it came back into style just so I could wear it again. My clothes were essential for work, my identity. Maybe to someone else, they were just a pile of cotton and elastic. But to me...it was all I had. Now I only owned the clothes on my back.

I didn't even have a pair of underwear.

I had two thousand dollars in my account, so I should be able to buy a couple of things, but I couldn't spend it all because I still had bills and I needed to eat.

How could those assholes steal from someone who was already poor?

Fucking terrible.

———

I WORKED all day and didn't tell anyone about the fact that I'd been robbed.

I didn't want their pity right now.

All I had left was my mother's picture, so I guess that gave those criminals some kind of conscience. I shouldn't be grateful they left it behind, but I was. It was the only thing I had left of my mother.

On my lunch break, I filed a report with the police, and they went to check on the apartment. Of course, they would find no leads, just an empty apartment. And when they asked if I had renters insurance, I had to tell the embarrassing truth —no. It wasn't because I wasn't responsible. It was simply because I couldn't afford it. It was the same reason I didn't have health insurance or a car with car insurance. I just couldn't swing it.

So now I was left with nothing.

New York was full of crime, and if these guys were brazen enough to steal a fridge in the middle of the night, they were brazen enough to do anything. Someone in my apartment complex must have been watching me because the thieves obviously knew I wouldn't be there all night. The probably watched my behaviors and figured out when I wouldn't be coming home until morning.

Made me sick to my stomach.

Maybe Slate was right. I couldn't continue to live there

anymore. I didn't want to spend my extra income toward higher rent. That would just put me in the same boat as before. But if I wanted to get out of the bad neighborhoods, I would have to fork over a lot of cash.

Fuck, I didn't know what to do.

————

I DIDN'T WANT to go to my apartment because there was nothing waiting for me there. I didn't even have a single piece of furniture to sit on. Going straight to Slate's place seemed most appealing, but since we weren't in a real relationship, I felt like that would be uncalled for.

So I bought a bottle of wine and sat on the kitchen counter as I drank it without a glass. I was still in the same clothes I wore the night before. I had my makeup and hair supplies in the bathroom because they were generous enough to leave those behind. I was able to take a shower and clean myself up before I pulled on the only outfit I had.

I should start moving on with my life by going shopping, but I was too depressed. I was already at rock-bottom, behaving like a prostitute just to clear my debt. And then, just when things started to get a little better, some assholes took all my shit. Now I would need money or donations to replace all of it.

Despite the sadness, there were still some things to be grateful for. For instance, I had a good job that paid well enough. What if I didn't have that? I really would have to be a prostitute. I also had my loans cleared, so now I was debt-free. That left a lot more money in my pocket. I also had my health.

So, it wasn't all bad…at least that's what I told myself.

My phone started to ring, and I noticed the battery was low. Of course, the jerks took my iPhone charger too…so I didn't even have that. I would have to make this conversation quick. But when I noticed Slate's name, I almost didn't answer.

I didn't want him to know what happened.

He would get pissed off and tell me he had been right all along—that I needed to move.

I hated it when he was right.

I sighed before I took the call. "Hi."

"Hey, Cherry."

"So, we're sticking with the nickname?"

"Do you not like it?"

I liked sweetheart, but that was a meaningless endearment, something you could say to a little girl. At least Cherry was more personal, more intimate. "No...I didn't say that."

"So, you do like it?"

"Maybe..."

He chuckled. "Want to have dinner with me tonight, Cherry?"

I certainly didn't want to sit in this apartment all night and feel sorry for myself. But I also didn't want to go out to dinner in the same outfit I wore yesterday. Slate would scream at me right in front of all the other patrons. "Can we eat at your place?"

"That's fine with me—as long as you're naked."

It was the one time where that request actually worked in my favor. "I can do that."

He paused at the sound of my compliance, because it was so unusual. "You're in a good mood today."

Or the complete opposite. "When do you want me to be there?"

"You can come by whenever. I just got out of the shower."

"Ooh...I'll hurry, then."

———

I WAS anxious to get to his place just so I had a comfortable

31

place to sit. I also didn't have to worry about those assholes watching me at his place. No one could bother me or rob me while I was there. I could also sleep that night without being scared.

I stepped out of the elevator and noticed him carrying the dishes to the table.

"You're right on time."

"Or you knew I was coming in the elevator."

He smiled then walked up to me to kiss me. His hand moved into my hair, and he gave me a tender embrace, a loving kiss, full of affection, the kind of kiss I needed after the shitty day I'd had.

He almost made me forget about it entirely.

When he pulled away, he noticed my outfit. "One, you aren't naked. And two, you're wearing the same outfit as before."

I didn't want to lie to him, but I also didn't want to tell him the truth. I wished I could just say nothing and deflect the conversation entirely.

When I didn't answer, his eyes narrowed.

"All my clothes are in the wash."

"At the laundry facility at your apartment? You're just going to leave them there?"

"The machine is broken, but the super can't fix it until tomorrow. So my clothes are locked in there."

His suspicion didn't subside. "And you're telling me *all* of your clothes are in the washer? I've seen your closet. It's huge."

Being the recipient of that hostile gaze told me I wasn't getting out of this alive. "What? I like this outfit. I can't wear it again?"

Like a volcano, he erupted—full of ash and fire. "Don't fucking lie to me." He crowded me, treating me like a mugger on the street that tried to rob him at gunpoint. Like I was his enemy, he forced me back, vicious and threatening. It was the scariest side of him I'd ever seen. With flared nostrils and wide eyes, he didn't act like I was the woman in his bed every night. "People don't lie to me because they know they can't get away with it. You aren't special. Now fucking tell me the truth."

I stepped back, afraid of his proximity rather than aroused by it. I dropped my chin because I didn't want to look at him when he was like this. I also didn't want to see his reaction when I told him the truth. "When I went home this morning…my place had been robbed."

He stilled in place, his breathing absent.

I kept looking at the floor because I was too scared to meet his gaze.

He said nothing, but his rage filled the air around us.

I couldn't stand the mystery, wondering what his features looked like, so I lifted my gaze to meet his.

He was terrifying.

"They took everything, even my fridge. The only thing they left behind was my makeup—"

"And you went inside?" he hissed.

"There was clearly no one there—"

"That was for the police to decide—not you. Did you call them?"

"Of course. They're working on it…"

"Do you have renters insurance?"

My answer was obvious, so I didn't bother saying it.

His nostrils flared once more. With a fury that couldn't be contained, he looked at me like he'd never been so disappointed. His limbs started to shake slightly so he stepped away, as if he needed space before he did something stupid. "I told you to move."

I crossed my arms over my chest.

"I told you to fucking move." He faced me again, his chest more muscular than usual because his skin was pumped full of blood and adrenaline.

"I'm not a millionaire who can just do whatever the hell I want."

"But you have no loans."

"But I haven't even been paid since you paid back my loans. Money doesn't grow on trees for me, Slate. My problems don't disappear, because I can't throw money at them. I do the best I can with the hand I was dealt. You wouldn't understand..."

"First of all, I'm a billionaire—"

"Wow...fuck you." I'd just had all my shit robbed, and he had the nerve to throw his wealth at me. I didn't even fantasize about being rich the way he was. I fantasized about having some security, like having a safe place to live and food on the table. I didn't dream of having a driver to take me everywhere.

His eyes flashed with hostility. "I'm a billionaire, which means I can help you."

"You've already helped me enough." He'd given me over six hundred thousand dollars to wipe my name clear of debt. I was the biggest donation he'd probably given all year.

"I never helped you. I paid for you—not the same thing at all."

"However you want to spin it, you've done enough." I wouldn't take a dime from him.

His anger was still at the forefront of his behavior, and it seemed like he wanted to strangle me with his large hands. "Then what will you do? What's your next plan?"

I shrugged. "Get a sleeping bag and wait until I get paid."

That was clearly the wrong thing to say, because he lost his shit. "Those motherfuckers could have broken in during the night and raped you. Do you understand that? They could have raped you then took all your stuff. Thank god you were at my place."

"I'm sure they waited until I was at your place before they made their move."

He took a sudden step backward, like he needed to restrain himself before he slapped me in the face. "And what if they didn't? What if they saw a beautiful woman all alone in her apartment and decided to take more than just your shit?" His arms stayed by his sides, the muscles twitching because there was so much fury in his blood.

"We can debate about that all night long, but it didn't happen."

"But it could have happened." He pointed his finger in my face. "And the fact that's even a possibility is unacceptable. You should have moved when I told you to move, and since you didn't, you're doing it now."

"I agree. I probably shouldn't stay there anymore—"

"Probably?" he snapped. "You can't stay there anymore. You'd better have a new place to live this week—and not in another shitty neighborhood. You need to get closer to the center of Manhattan."

"No such thing in my price range, unless I get some roommates. And even then, we'll have two girls per room. I'd rather live in a dump alone than share my space. I'm twenty-three years old. I shouldn't be living with someone."

"Then you'll have to make it work."

"Even with my loans gone, that's nearly impossible."

"You better figure something out. If you think I'm gonna let this go, I'm not."

No, I knew better than that.

As if he couldn't stand to look at me anymore, he walked back to the table and sat down. He picked up his fork and stared at his food without taking a bite.

Once it seemed like his hostility had dimmed, I joined him at the table.

He didn't move, staring at his food like an immobile statue.

I tried to keep things light by taking a bite. "This is good."

"So they took all your clothes too?"

I guess the conversation wasn't over. "Yeah...they took it all."

He shook his head and poked at his food with the fork. "Fucking disgusting."

"Yeah..."

"It's someone in your complex. Someone watching when you come and go."

I'd come to the same conclusion.

"You aren't going back there." He lifted his head this time and looked me in the eye.

"Well, it's where I live. So I have to go back there."

"You're staying with me until we get this figured out. I'm not letting you sleep on the floor like some kind of homeless person, vulnerable to the jackasses watching you from across the way. They crossed you, which means they crossed me. I'm not letting them bother you again."

I didn't want his charity, but I couldn't deny that staying with him was a dream come true. It was the safest place in the world, on the top story of his building with a strong man beside me in that enormous bed. I wouldn't have to sleep with one eye open.

"There's nothing in the apartment anyway. No reason to stay there."

"I feel bad infringing on your space."

"Don't. As long as you're fucking me, I don't care. If you're sick of me, there're 7,000 square feet where you can disappear."

Even at his worst, I couldn't get sick of him.

"I have to be honest. It's probably going to be a while before I get a new place."

"We decided on a week."

"And that's unrealistic."

"Why?" He finally took a bite of his food, now that it was cold.

"Because I need to save up to buy new furniture. I don't

have anything. And I'll have to replace the fridge that was stolen."

"But that wasn't your fridge."

"But it was included in my lease, and I don't have renters insurance."

He abandoned his food once more and set down his fork. "Then you get an apartment with no furniture—for the time being."

"How is that any different than my current situation?"

"It'll be a safer apartment."

"Shouldn't I wait until I can afford a bed first? A couch, maybe? Some silverware?"

"I think your safety is more important than inanimate objects."

"But those objects cost money."

"Then you can make do without them. Or put everything on a credit card."

Now that I didn't have any debt, it was possible I could extend my line of credit and get the things I needed. But getting a nice apartment would be a challenge to begin with. Unless I put all of my income toward rent, I would never be able to afford it. And I needed to start thinking about retirement and the future. There were other things more important than having a nice place to live. For instance, I really needed to get some health insurance. Life was good until something terrible happened to you, and without that special card, it could be life-and-death. "I understand you care about me, but it's gonna be a while for me to figure this out. I need to find a good place to live, but I need to put money aside for savings, emergencies, health insurance—"

"Renters insurance."

"Among other things…" I took another bite of my food. "I'm just letting you know this isn't so simple. I only have a certain budget, and I can't spend it all to live in the nicest place possible. That's just impractical. You're a logical man, and you must realize that."

He stared at his food and took a bite. "Don't expect me to be rational right now. Some fuckers are watching your every move. All I want is for you to be safe. Until I know you're safe, I can't see me being rational whatsoever. So you're staying here until we get this figured out. Don't argue with me about it."

———

I WORE his clothes to bed that night and wasn't sure what I would wear tomorrow. All I had was that single outfit I'd been wearing for the last two days in a row. If I walked into the office like that, people would definitely notice. I could say I was trying to be environmentally friendly by not washing my clothes, but people probably wouldn't believe me.

I wasn't sure what I was going to do.

It's not like I could hit up a clothing store on the way to work.

I would just have to face the humiliation—and tell the truth.

Slate got into bed beside me, but he kept his boxers on like sex wasn't on the menu. He moved into my back and spooned me from behind, his dick soft against my backside. He would normally be hard touching me like this, but his arousal was nonexistent for the evening.

Even if he didn't want to be physical with me, just having him there was nice. His powerful arms wrapped around me and protected me from the terrors outside his walls. His fortress was impenetrable, unconquerable. He would never let anything happen to me, not now and not ever.

His deep voice broke the silence. "I want you to end your lease at your apartment. Just end it now. We'll figure out what to do later."

———

WHEN I WOKE up the next morning, Slate was already in the shower.

I was up earlier than usual because the sound of the running water disturbed me. I had such a great night of sleep last night, probably because of the strong man who was beside me all night, so I didn't want to get out of bed. I rubbed the sleep from my eyes before I ventured into the living room and tracked down the coffee.

Laid out across the table was women's clothing, high-end fashion pieces I could never afford. There were jeans and tops, along with cute coats, scarfs, boots, and my dream dresses. There were five outfits altogether, one for every day of the week. Slate never had women at his apartment, so I knew they had to be for me.

He came up behind me, the towel wrapped around his waist. "I had my maid pick those up for you."

Since I worked in fashion, I recognized every single brand that was lying on the table. All high-end stuff I could never afford—even without my loans haunting me. I'd always been a bargain shopper, and now I would walk into my office with more money on my body than I had in my bank account. "This is for me?" I asked incredulously, looking at the plastic sheath that protected the clothes.

"You can't wear the same outfit until you get paid."

"But you didn't need to get me Louis Vuitton and Chanel..."

He shrugged. "I don't know much about fashion. I just wear what my girl gets me."

"Your girl?" I asked, unable to keep the jealousy out of my voice.

"My personal shopper. I described your body to her, and this is what she came up with." He walked into the kitchen in the towel and made himself a pot of coffee. "Do I look like a man who goes shopping when he gets off work?" He came back to me, holding two mugs of steaming coffee.

I took the mug and smelled the freshly ground coffee that was so luxurious, I didn't even know such nice things existed. I used Folgers, the big red can with pounds of ground coffee. And most of the time, I brewed the same batch twice just to save some money. This was high-quality stuff, freshly roasted beans that had just been ground. As if the sexy man weren't enough to get me to crash here for a while, the coffee could definitely get me to stay. "I appreciate the gesture, but I don't need expensive clothes. I never wear stuff like this."

"Well, now you do." He sipped his coffee as he watched me with eyes that matched the brew in his hand. He'd just shaved his jawline, so his beautiful complexion was more visible. He had the most masculine features, prominent cheekbones, full lips, and constant hostility in his gaze.

"But I don't want you to spend this kind of money on me."

"It's really of no consequence."

"But I don't want your money. When I shop, I'm a bargain hunter. I wait until things go on sale a million times before I buy anything."

"Well, we don't have time for that. So shut that pretty mouth and get ready for work."

"Shut that pretty mouth?" I asked, my hands moving to my hips.

He took another drink before he set the mug on the table. "I'm not in the mood today, Cherry. Get dressed and go to work."

3

Slate

I SPOKE TO MY PI OVER THE SPEAKERPHONE. "IT HAPPENED a few nights ago. They cleaned her out completely. I want to know who was responsible. I want names and addresses. Then I'm going to kill every single one of them. You understand?"

"Got it." James hung up.

I listened to the line go dead as I stared out of the glass walls that surrounded my office. My assistants had a barrier behind them, so they couldn't look into my personal space while they were on the clock. It gave me some privacy, to sit there and mull over my thoughts when I wasn't working.

I was too pissed off to focus right now.

I'd told her to move—more than once. She lived in a sketchy area, and of course, a beautiful woman like that had eyes on her no matter where she lived. In her universe, that was all she could afford, so it was justifiable. She didn't have a lot of options, so she wasn't concerned about her safety.

But I was concerned.

I missed the way my life used to be, when I fucked women in one of my hotels then never saw them again. I never asked why they needed to sell their virginity. I never allowed myself any reason to care. I fucked them roughly like an asshole, then walked out the door, forgetting their name the second I finished my shower. It was heartless and cold, but it made my life easier.

Now I had this woman living with me because she had nowhere else to go.

I didn't want her going back to that dump of an apartment, especially when the thieves were probably still watching her, seeing that she had no one to turn to, so she slept in a sleeping bag on the floor. They would laugh at her, mock her.

I couldn't let that happen.

She wasn't my responsibility, but the idea of abandoning her made me sick to my stomach.

Sometimes I lost touch with reality when it came to money. I didn't have many problems because everything could be solved with a wad of cash. To me, it should be simple for her to move to a good part of Manhattan, to have a place with a doorman and a passcode. But then I realized not everyone lived the way I did—especially her. Even with her debt wiped away, she really stood no chance. Any luxurious place in Manhattan was going to cost at least ten grand a month, and there was no possibility she could ever afford that.

But I didn't want her to leave in another dump. A woman like her should be safe, should be protected.

How would I make that happen?

She couldn't live with me forever. That was nonnegotiable. I needed my space and my privacy. She'd just started sleeping over, which was also a first for me. Sometimes she felt like my girlfriend rather than my fuck buddy, and that was already too much.

So what was the solution?

How did I keep her safe without bringing us closer together?

There was no answer.

Jillian's voice shattered my thoughts over the intercom. "Sir, your brother has just returned to the office."

The honeymoon was over already? "Is she with him?"

"Yes."

I rolled my eyes. "Thanks for letting me know."

———

I SHOULD HAVE KNOWN they would return from their honeymoon eventually. Time went by too fast, and now I didn't just have a dumb-ass brother to deal with, but a psychopathic sister-in-law.

I wasn't sure if I could even call her my sister-in-law.

She was just Simone...the gold-digging bitch.

Jillian spoke through the intercom. "Your brother is here to see you, sir."

I was hoping we would avoid each other for a few more weeks. "Send him in."

Coen stepped through the glass door a moment later, noticeably tanned with a black wedding ring on his left hand. He wore a black suit and tie, and despite the vacation he'd just had, he looked stressed. "Slate."

I didn't rise from my seat to shake his hand. "Coen. How was the honeymoon?"

"No complaints." He stood at my desk and didn't take a seat. His hands slid into his pockets as he hovered above me. "Anything you need to share with me?"

"I had Jillian drop off all the paperwork this morning."

"I got it. Wasn't sure if you wanted to add something."

If I had, I would have included it in the paperwork. Any extended interaction with my brother was borderline torture. He was just a stranger, a pain in the ass. As time passed, I liked him less and less. I didn't respect him as a man, and that was the worst thing you could lose—respect.

"Mother wants us to get together for dinner tonight."

They'd only been gone a week. Did we need to get together to hear about the drinking and fucking? "When

Mother's gone, we won't be doing this bullshit anymore. So how about we stop doing this bullshit now?" I looked him in the eye and didn't feel slightly apologetic for what I said. I meant it with every fiber of my being. I already had to deal with his pussy-ass at work, and now I had to have a meal with him like we were family.

He tilted his chin toward the ground as if he were deflecting the insult. "I think it would mean a lot to Mother."

"And since when did you start caring about other people's feelings?"

Stoic, he lifted his gaze and watched me. There was a long stretch of silence, as if he couldn't find a single justification to sidestep the insult. "Mother said she's getting her floors waxed and her carpets cleaned. Wanted to know if we could do it at your place."

My brother had been to my apartment once. Simone never had. I didn't want to open the door to my enemies, but I'd rather have them on my turf than go to theirs. Now that Monroe was temporarily living with me, I had an ally on my side of the table. "That's fine."

"Tonight?"

"That's short notice."

"You know Mother. She gets anxious."

"Yes…indeed."

———

MONROE WORKED IN MIDTOWN, so she only had a five-minute walk to my penthouse.

I got home before she did, but I worked out upstairs then took a shower so I didn't see her. When I was finished getting ready, I found her sitting on the couch, wearing the Louis Vuitton outfit my maid had dropped off.

"Hey." Her eyes lit up when she saw me, like she'd been looking forward to seeing me all day. She left the couch and moved into my chest to kiss me, to kiss me the way a lover greeted her man when he stepped through the door. She rose on her tiptoes and wrapped her arms around my neck.

I squeezed the small of her back, enjoying the sight of her the second I stepped into the living room. Maybe having her live with me wouldn't be so bad after all. "You're in a good mood." I pulled away and looked down into her beautiful face, relieved she was somewhere safe where no one could bother her again.

"Not particularly. Just happy to see you."

I looked her outfit up and down, liking her thigh-high boots and her skintight long-sleeved black dress. "You look beautiful in that."

"Well, of course I do. It's Louis Vuitton."

"Then aren't you glad I bought it for you?"

"Yes…but you really didn't need to do that." She pulled away, growing self-conscious when I reminded her I was the one who paid for the clothes on her back.

Not that I was trying to make her feel bad about that. "I have some bad news."

"What kind of bad news?"

"My family is coming over tonight for dinner. That means I need to start cooking."

"Your family?" she asked in surprise. "Your brother is back from his honeymoon?"

"Unfortunately."

"I guess I can hang at a friend's house until your evening is over."

I gave her an incredulous look. "Why would you do that?"

"Isn't this a family thing?"

"Yes. But you live here. Of course you're invited."

"Really?"

"I took you to my brother's wedding, but staying for dinner is too much?" I teased.

"I thought maybe you wanted some private time," she

45

said with a shrug. "Are you going to tell them I was robbed and I'm living here temporarily?"

"I'm not telling them anything. My private life is none of their business."

"Well, they're your family. They're going to be curious."

I walked into the kitchen and opened the fridge to see all the ingredients I'd asked my maid to pick up at the store. I was making grilled lemon chicken with veggies and cauliflower rice. My mother and brother had strict diets too, probably because my father died too young of a heart attack. Simone was a stick, so she didn't eat carbs either. "I don't care how curious they are."

She eyed the food as I set everything on the counter. "Another carb-free meal? So the whole family is perpetually boring?"

"Not boring. Just picky."

"You aren't even making real rice. Just cauliflower rice."

"It's good. Have you ever had it?"

"No…"

"Then you'll see how good it is."

"I guess so. How can I help?"

"I'll take care of the food. How about you set the table?"

"I can do that."

I only had an hour to get everything ready, so I watched Monroe prepare the kitchen table, the bottles of wine, and the linen napkins as I cooked the chicken on the stove and prepared the sides at the same time.

Monroe returned to the kitchen. "Does that mean Gold Digger will be here?"

"Is that what we're calling her now?"

"You've got a better name?" she countered.

I grinned. "I guess I don't."

She pulled the dishes out of the cabinet then placed them on the counter so I could scoop the food onto each dish. Then she covered each one with foil and placed them in the preheated oven. "They'll stay warm until they—"

The elevator beeped as my mother's voice came through the speaker. "We're punctual, as always."

"Never mind." She pulled the dishes out of the oven and ripped off the foil.

I washed my hands before I hit the button on the elevator and allowed them to rise to my floor.

Monroe came to my side. "I'm nervous."

"You've met them before."

"Yeah, but I really hate Simone."

"Simone is just a bitch. My brother is the one you should hate."

"No." She shook her head. "I know things aren't great between you, but I know your brother loves you... It's just hidden under many bad decisions."

The elevator stopped and the doors opened.

My mother stepped inside with a teal shawl tossed over her shoulder. In nude heels with skinny jeans and a purple blouse, she looked ready for the runway rather than a midweek family dinner. "Something smells wonderful." She kissed me on the cheek before she turned to Monroe. "Oh, sweetheart. I was hoping you would be here." She hugged her hard before she admired her outfit. "You look stunning, by the way. I love this."

My brother came in next, Simone lingering beside him. "Slate."

"Coen." I gave him a curt nod, like he was a stranger. I somehow managed to greet Simone even more coldly. "Simone. You guys both look tan from the honeymoon."

"We laid out in the sun most of the time." She hardly looked at me because she was staring at Monroe the entire time, her eyebrow raised and her interest engaged. "Someone got a makeover."

I could hardly tolerate Simone when she disrespected me,

but I couldn't tolerate it at all if she disrespected Monroe. "This is a two-way street, Simone. I can make your life a living hell too. Keep that in mind."

Monroe greeted my brother. "I hope you had a great time on your honeymoon." She shook his hand, being polite without being overly affectionate.

"We did," Coen answered. "Thank you."

Monroe turned to Simone next, but she didn't recoil in fear like most other women would. "Nice to see you again. The Bahamas gave you a perfect glow."

"That glow is just from happiness," Simone said. "Not the sun." She hooked her arm through Coen's and stepped farther inside the apartment.

Monroe turned to me, her eyebrow raised. Then she mouthed, "Bi-otch."

I tried not to laugh.

Mother noticed the exchange but didn't comment on it. "What smells so good?"

"Cauliflower rice."

"Good," Mother said. "One of my favorites. I should have recognized it from the smell."

Monroe headed to the bar and started serving drinks. "What can I get you? We have red, white, scotch—"

Simone cut her off like she was an incompetent waitress. "Water with lemon."

How did she manage to be a bitch all the time? Had she been that bad when we were together? "I'll get it, Monroe. Everyone else will have white wine."

4

Monroe

SIMONE WAS A BIGGER BITCH THAN I REMEMBERED. Now that she was officially Mrs. Remington, she didn't seem to care about hiding her true colors. She displayed them brightly, like they were the hues of the rainbow—except they were ugly shades.

Now I really did think less of Coen for putting up with a woman who became a snob overnight. I hardly knew her, and even I could tell all she wanted was a life of luxury and riches. She didn't bother showing any respect to his own family, like they were beneath her the second she took his name.

My eyes kept drifting back to Slate, knowing he was counting down the minutes until this horrifying dinner was over. All Simone did was complain about how dry the chicken was, and then she bragged about how nice their honeymoon was, even though she didn't spend a dime on it.

If Slate and I, as well as Slate's mother, could see her true nature, how could Coen be so blind to it?

My sympathy was starting to wane.

Once dinner was finished, I cleared the plates and took them to the sink, mainly just so I wouldn't have to hear Simone's obnoxious voice so loudly. Once I was confined in

49

the kitchen, the echoes of conversation drifted away slightly, allowing me to hear my thoughts once again. They said money changed people, but I thought money only enhanced people. She was always a bitch, but now she felt like she had enough power that she didn't need to hide her true self anymore.

Poor Slate. All of his fears had been warranted.

I rinsed the dishes just so I had something to do, anything that could stall for time. It was the middle of the week, so his family couldn't be staying here that much longer.

"Don't you have a maid for that?" Simone's obnoxious tone came from behind me as she placed her water glass on the counter beside me.

"I don't mind helping."

She leaned against the counter and looked at me, her arms crossed over her chest. "I fired Coen's old maid. Took orders from him a lot better than she took them from me."

"Well, maids aren't supposed to take orders." I kept my eyes on my hands as I rinsed the crumbs down the drain. "They aren't slaves, Simone. They're human beings...in case you haven't noticed." Growing up poor my whole life made me despise women like Simone. They didn't want money for security, just to oppress those with no power. She got off on it, inflated her ego.

She watched me with the same sinister expression a snake would display. "I'm guessing Money Bags bought this little ensemble for you." She pointed from my shoulder down to my feet. "Those boots alone are at least twenty-five hundred dollars—and I suspect you don't have that."

"I suspect you wouldn't either—without Coen's money." Maybe Slate had to be civil to her, but I certainly didn't. I wasn't going to let a bully walk all over me and put me down like she had the right.

Her eyes darkened. "Stupid people are always brave."

"And arrogant people are always careless." I turned off

the faucet and faced her head on, unintimidated by her beauty and confidence. "The least you could do is treat Coen's family with respect. You aren't even trying—and that's just cold."

"You aren't his family."

"I'm not talking about me, blondie," I snapped. "You're making it so obvious that you're only with him for his money. If you're willing to ruin a man's life and reputation just for cash...then nothing in this world will ever truly make you happy. And you know what? I feel sorry for you." I turned away and stacked the dishes in the dishwasher.

She watched me, her eyes cold as ice. "You're one to talk. Maybe I like money, but I wouldn't sell my virginity just to get it. You think you're better than me—but at least I'm not a whore."

———

SIMONE LEFT without saying goodbye to me, but Elizabeth showed me far more affection than she did her own daughter-in-law. I was always given a kiss on the cheek and a hug that reminded me of the way my mother used to hold me.

They all stepped into the elevator then disappeared, Simone shooting daggers with her eyes.

The doors shut, and they finally left our sight.

Slate turned to me, his observant gaze full of accusation. "What happened?"

"What makes you think anything happened?"

"Because Simone has nukes in her eyes." Slate hadn't acted like anything was out of the ordinary while his family was there, but now that it was just the two of us, he was frank. "I know you guys were alone in the kitchen together."

"She's a nightmare. That's what happened."

"I could have told you that." He turned away and cleared the remaining glasses from the table.

"I told her to show some respect to Coen's family and at least pretend she wasn't a gold digger… She didn't like that very much."

Slate paused as he looked at me. "You said that to her face?"

"Yeah." Now that I looked at it with hindsight, it didn't seem very smart. "She said she fired Coen's old maid because she wasn't obedient enough, then put me down because you bought me these clothes… I couldn't stand there. I've met some bitches in my life, and since I work at a fashion line, I've had more than my fair share. But she's…something else." I couldn't believe that Slate had ever been with her in the first place. He seemed too smart for that.

"I'm glad there's someone who hates her more than I do."

"I just hate when rich people treat regular people like garbage. I've been poor all my life, and I hate feeling helpless and insignificant. She's the kind of person who wants to abuse her power, who doesn't care how the company treats her employees. She's selfish and greedy. I hate people like that." Slate had never been that way, even if he was a little arrogant about his wealth sometimes. It was nothing compared to Simone—and at least he worked for it. "And then…she said something pretty interesting."

"Which is?" He stood next to the table in a t-shirt under a gray cardigan, looking like a model in a fall catalog.

"Somehow, she knows I sold my virginity to you."

Slate was quiet as he absorbed this information, like his brain couldn't soak it in right away. He stepped closer to me, still slowly processing it. "She said that?"

I nodded.

"And what did you say?"

"Nothing. She walked out."

"Did she say how she knew that?"

I shook my head. "No. But she seemed pretty confident her claim was true."

Still bewildered, he shifted his eyes back and forth as he processed what I'd said. "I have no idea how she found out."

"Neither do I." I hadn't told a soul, except for Wyatt. But I didn't see how there could be a link between the two of them. "If you're her enemy, I guess it's not surprising that she's keeping tabs on you."

"But she must have hired a PI."

"She wants to make sure she has dirt on you if you make a move against her."

Slate abandoned the tablecloth and the leftover glasses and looked at me instead. "That does sound like something she would do. But she's also stupid if she thinks I care what my mother and brother think of me." He crossed his arms over his chest and continued to look fearless, like his darkest secret wasn't in the wrong hands.

"She probably knows I'm not the first cherry you paid for."

"No, I'm sure she knows everything." While he didn't appear afraid, he did seem uncomfortable. "There's nothing she could do to my reputation because that's already been destroyed—when she made a fool out of me. But I don't want her to drag your name through the mud."

"I'm a nobody, so no problem there." I didn't have a famous name. I was just some person in a city full of millions of people.

"But that doesn't mean it won't turn you into somebody. Your colleagues might find out about it, and it could follow you everywhere you go. I don't want that to happen to you." He dropped his arms and picked up the rest of the dishes before he carried everything to the sink.

I followed him into the kitchen. "I'm not scared of her."

"She's petty and unpredictable. As much as I hate to admit it...we should be scared of her." He washed his hands before he turned back to me, leaving most of the dishes untouched in the bottom of the sink. "She'll hold this information over my head to keep me in line. But I don't negotiate with terrorists, so her little plan won't work so well."

"Good." I would rather be free with the truth than hidden away with a lie.

"I guess I don't want my mother to know… She'd be disappointed in me." He leaned against the counter and gripped the edge with both hands, his muscular body sexy no matter how he held himself. "Not to mention, that would just be awkward."

"Yeah…it would be. So what are you going to do?"

He shrugged. "I'm not going to let her walk all over me. That's for sure."

"I expected nothing less."

"But I don't know what to do about you…" He looked me in the eye with those deep wells of oil, full of murky handsomeness.

"Don't worry about me."

"I don't want her to tarnish your reputation. It's different for a woman."

I shrugged. "It'll just show me who my real friends are."

He smiled slightly. "Are you always this brave, or are you just a good actress?"

"Neither. I just hate Simone to the exclusion of all else." She strutted into every room like she owned it. She treated all of us like we were maids rather than company. That woman had gotten far by playing tricks, and I didn't want her to go any further. She needed to be knocked down—once and for all. "Seeing the way she treats your family really pisses me off. And it's hard for me to sympathize with Coen when it's so glaringly obvious. There's no way he's unaware of how terrible she is."

He shrugged. "I don't get it either. It's hard to believe that Coen used to be a cool guy. We used to go out every weekend, play basketball, the whole nine yards. But all of that changed when she cast her spell."

I could hear the silent sadness in his voice, the pain from losing his brother. It seemed like Coen was dead, even though he was still among the living. His positive attributes were only spoken of in the past tense, like all those memories had been buried a long time ago. "Maybe she'll divorce him and disappear."

"She will divorce him, but she'll never disappear. She'll get what she wants and torture us for the rest of our lives."

"I can't believe someone would do that…for money." If a person was willing to stoop that low for cash, it made me wonder how unhappy they were. They were willing to strip away their integrity, honesty, and humanity just to have a fat bank account. It was awful.

"I'll believe anything at this point…because I've seen it all." He left the kitchen and walked past the dining table on the way to bed.

I followed him and left the mess behind so the maid could take care of it tomorrow.

Slate stripped off his clothes and left a pile on the floor to be dealt with later. He ran his fingers through his short black hair before he set the alarm on his bedside. He stood in his boxers as his perfectly chiseled chest expanded with every breath he took. Like a living statue, he was all beauty and strength.

I got into bed in just my panties, knowing it would be pointless to pull on a t-shirt.

When he was done with his phone, he pushed down his boxers then got into bed naked.

The lights were off, and we were finally surrounded by silence. The echoes from the earlier conversation with his family had died away, and now this horrible night was officially a memory.

But his bad mood didn't destroy his arousal. He grabbed my arm then rolled me onto my stomach as his heavy body pressed me into the mattress. He covered me entirely, his fists making the mattress sink directly underneath us. After he pulled down my panties, he slicked the head of his cock and pressed himself inside me.

He didn't take me slowly and gently like he had the past few weeks. Now he just wanted to fuck me, to get exactly what he paid for. His hand gripped my neck, and he lifted my chin up so my back would straighten. Then he slowly descended inside me, a tighter fit because my legs were closed. He sank deep until his balls touched my skin. A light moan filled the darkness as he held himself on top of me, balls deep inside my cunt.

He pressed his mouth to my ear and breathed quietly as he enjoyed me, his cock throbbing with happiness. The slight twitches felt like the beat of a drum because his dick was so large. It was like a sword, and I was a sheath. It could rip me in two if he pushed too hard. "I'll still take it easy on you… because it's so deep." He started to thrust, his large cock hitting me at the most intimate angle possible.

I moaned when I felt my body jerk forward. I was completely full, his enormous cock stretching me in every way imaginable. It was so big, so solid, and it was a miracle I had stretched out enough to take him like this.

He moved quicker than usual but not at a speed I couldn't handle. His thrusts weren't violent like they'd been before. He carefully tapped his balls on the bed as he kept going, keeping a fluid pace that was easy for me to enjoy.

He leaned over me and looked into my face, dominating me like a country he'd just seized. He kept me pinned beneath him, like he owned me in every way he could. His breathing escalated, and he ground his hips into my ass, forcing my clit to rub against the sheets underneath me.

It was a position we'd never tried before, but I enjoyed it just the way I did with missionary. I gripped the sheets in front of me and felt his thick dick pierce me over and over again.

"Come, Cherry. Before I fuck this pretty little asshole instead." His deep voice reminded me how sexy he was, that he was a strong and muscular man deep inside me even though I couldn't see him. His dick throbbed like he didn't want to wait a second longer, and I was the only reason he couldn't enjoy himself.

His voice made me tighten. His dick made me clench. The feeling of his hips against my ass made me come apart. Thoughts of dinner were long gone as I gripped the sheets and came around his cock, closing my eyes and screaming into the darkness.

The instant he felt my release, he let go. He thrust violently as he finished, injecting my pussy with mounds of his come. He growled under his breath, dumping pile upon pile of his seed into my tiny slit. "Yes…" He held himself still, savoring the euphoric sensation between his legs.

Now I came every night before bed, and every orgasm was just as good as the previous one. Slate pleased himself, but he pleased me at the same time. I didn't have a place to live and my life was in ruins, but since I had this man between my legs every night, it didn't feel so bad.

He pulled out of me slowly to make sure he'd left all of his arousal behind. His lips found my shoulder, and he gave me a hard kiss before he rolled over to his side of the bed.

I stayed in my position as I felt his heavy come inside me. The memory of the orgasm was still sparkling in my skull, and I enjoyed the lingering effects as I caught my breath, my pussy so satisfied from such an animalistic position.

He slapped his palm against my ass. "Go to bed, Cherry." He lay on his back with his face focused on the ceiling.

I was tired a minute ago, but now that I was satisfied and stuffed with his come, I didn't want to go anywhere. I wanted to stay right there and feel his massive body on top of me. "Could we do that again?"

After a long pause, he turned his head toward me, the

arousal already replacing the satisfaction in his eyes. "You like it like that, Cherry?"

"Yes."

He moved onto his arms again before placing kisses against the back of my neck and all the way down my spine. "Then I'll give it to you as many times as you want."

5

Slate

Days passed, and I shared my space with Monroe. She was there every day when I came home from work, and she was there before I left in the morning. The solitude I used to have in this penthouse was nonexistent, filled with her laughs, moans, and sometimes snores.

I picked up more clothes for her because she had limited supplies, and before long, she had her own section in my closet.

I stood in front of it as I examined my suits, seeing the dresses, skirts, and boots that filled her small space. Everything was in fall colors because of the time of year. My closet used to smell like fresh linen and cologne, but now it smelled like Monroe's perfume.

This was the last thing I ever wanted—to live with a woman.

But now I did.

She wasn't my girlfriend so it wasn't my responsibility to take care of her, but leaving her to fend for herself in this harsh world wasn't an option. She was far too innocent to handle cruelty. It didn't seem like she had many friends either. And she certainly didn't have any family.

I was all she had.

But living together for months wasn't a solution I could accept. It would make her get attached to me, make her want more from me. She already made demands in the bedroom instead of fulfilling her obligation, so it was obvious she had more power than she should.

I couldn't let myself fall into a black hole. Once I was inside, I would never be able to climb back out.

She stepped into the bedroom behind me, dressed in leggings and a workout bra. "Your gym is nice."

My thoughts were shattered as I stared into the contents of my closet and looked for a t-shirt. I grabbed an olive green one and pulled it on. "Thank you."

"It's nice to work out alone. You never have to worry about people bothering you."

People didn't bother me anyway. As if they would be dumb enough to say anything to me.

"I think the last time I worked out was in high school, so I'm a bit out of shape." Sweat glistened on her forehead, and strands of her hair were slightly loose from her ponytail. Her black leggings fit her sculpted legs perfectly, and her sports bra pushed her tits together nicely. For someone who never worked out, she sure looked like it.

"You don't look out of shape to me." I turned to her, aroused by the sweat on her shoulders and arms rather than deterred by it. It reminded me of sex, how hot and sweaty she would get when she bounced up and down on my length.

"Sex is the only exercise I get, and that didn't start until recently."

"And it clearly whipped you into shape. Maybe we should even step it up a little."

She narrowed her eyes playfully. "You just said I was in shape."

"But everyone could use a little improvement." I stepped closer to her and looked at the sweat that shone on her chest and in her cleavage. I wanted to cup both of her tits in my hand and slide my dick through those soft globes. It'd been a while since I tit-fucked someone, and I'd never seen a pair of tits I wanted to fuck more.

She placed her fingers under my chin and lifted my gaze. "My eyes are up here."

I grabbed her wrist and yanked her fingers from my face. "Your eyes are wherever I want them to be." I gripped her sports bra and pulled it over her head, revealing the rack I hadn't stopped thinking about since she'd walked into the room.

She gave me a playful wink before she strode into the bathroom, her ass shaking as she moved.

I watched her turn the corner before I pulled my fresh shirt over my head and followed her. The water was already running, and steam filled the room. My jeans and boxers hit the floor as I stared at her naked body behind the glass door. Her sexy skin was slick with the warm water, her long legs sexy and smooth. She had the perfect hourglass figure, a gorgeous waist with ample tits. She was the kind of woman that made me feel like a real man—a caveman. All I thought about was sex and domination when I looked at her. I wanted to hide her in my cave while I hunted for food and resources. Then I wanted to come back to her and fuck her like an animal.

I stepped under the warm water with her.

"I thought you already showered." She tilted her head back and let the water soak her hair. It clung to the back of her neck and trailed down her spine.

"I could use another." My palms immediately went for her tits, and I squeezed them both hard, my thumbs testing the firmness of her nipples. Anytime this woman was in the same room with me, all I could think about was sex, hot and violent sex. It didn't matter how many beautiful women I saw on the street, she was the only woman I wanted to fuck. She was the only woman who got me so hard, it was like I'd taken a week's worth of Viagra. "Bend over."

"Where?" she asked like a smartass.

"Here." I gripped her waist and turned her around before I forced her body to bend. "Hands against the wall."

She pressed her palms against the wall and arched her back, making her ass stick out as she supported herself with her hands.

I grabbed the high-pressure shower head off the mount then pressed it right against her clit.

"Oh…" She tensed when she felt the water hit her clit at incredible velocity, warm and inviting. She arched her back farther and tilted her head back, obviously never having experienced something like this before.

It was easy to get my dick inside because her pussy was so relaxed. Even with the water adding friction, I was able to shove myself inside her with almost no restriction. "Your cunt is finally molding to me." I gripped her shoulder and kept her still as I fucked her roughly from behind. I kept the shower head right against her clit, making her body tense and writhe as I fucked her hard like I'd fantasized.

Her cries echoed off the shower walls, and within thirty seconds, she came around me, the hot water driving her into a climax that made her scream at the top of her lungs. Her hands dragged down the wall as she thrust back into me, the pleasure forcing her body to take my dick harder.

"You like that, Cherry?" My fingers dug into her shoulder as I kept her still and fucked her, my ass tightening and my balls swinging. I pressed the shower head tighter against her, putting it in a special place that she couldn't control.

"Yes…"

"Hold it." I let her take the shower head so I could hold on to her with both hands. I gripped her hips and thrust into her harder than before, driving my dick so deep inside her that she would be sore the second we were finished.

She kept the shower head against her body and came a minute later, the pressure doing all the work so I could enjoy her.

When I felt the flood of arousal surround my dick, I couldn't hold on any longer. I used to pride myself on my impressive endurance, but ever since being with her, I seemed to last a shorter time with every single fuck. The second she came, I didn't want to keep going. I wanted to explode and feel the same pleasure. I tugged on her hips and came inside her, moaning as I felt my seed shoot out and hit her deep. My fingertips dug into her skin, and I moaned as I finished, feeling so much satisfaction from an act I'd been doing with hundreds of women for well over a decade.

But with her, it felt particularly good.

I stayed inside her until I was completely done, fully embedded in that small pussy I destroyed with my large size. I slowly pulled out, the head of my cock dripping with my seed. The shower immediately washed it away, but I could see the come flowing from her entrance.

I admired my handiwork with a slight smile.

She straightened then returned the shower head to its metal stand. Her legs were wobbly, and she held the wall for balance as she righted herself. Her playfulness was absent now that she was satisfied. All her energy had disappeared, replaced by exhaustion.

"Never used a shower head like that?" I asked, knowing the answer without her response.

"Can't say I have…"

"Well, it looks like you met your new best friend."

"My second best friend." She glanced at my dick. "I already have a first."

―――――

WHEN WE SAT down to dinner, I pulled out all the listings

I'd printed out. "I found a few apartments I think you'll like." As far as I could tell, it didn't seem like she'd been on the hunt for a new place to live. My penthouse was the epitome of luxury so it wasn't surprising that she didn't want to leave, but she certainly couldn't live there.

She glanced at the papers, a slight look of disappointment on her face.

She'd been living with me for almost two weeks, and while it was a pleasure having her here, she couldn't stay much longer.

She set down her utensils and looked through the pages.

I picked the cheapest places I could find on this side of town. Most of them were broom closets, but they were still affordable. "They are all available now, so whatever one you want, it's yours."

She flipped through all the pages before she tossed them onto the table. "Slate, I can't afford any of these."

"Yes, you can."

"I can technically afford these, but I'd have no money for anything else."

"Well, what's more important? Being safe or having extra money?"

"It's not about having extra money," she snapped. "It's about affording health insurance and food. Not everyone is a billionaire like you."

"These apartments aren't billions of dollars."

"They may as well be because I can't afford them. I can barely afford Brooklyn. If you really want me to leave, you need to suggest practical places. If I move in to one of these apartments, I'm gonna be just as poor as I was at my old place."

"And safe—"

"No, Slate. If you really want me out, I can stay with a colleague until I get settled."

"It's not that I want you out."

"I think it is. And if that's the case, just tell me. I don't want to overstay my welcome."

I didn't want her to live with me, but I didn't want her to stay somewhere else. I didn't trust whoever she stayed with, and after everything she'd been through, I wanted her to feel comfortable. Ever since she stepped foot inside my door, she was noticeably calmer, more relaxed. "I just want you to find a nice place."

"Unless I get a huge promotion, that's not going to happen."

I didn't want her getting farther away from Manhattan, staying in another dumpy place just so the past could repeat itself. A woman like her should be protected, should be kept safe like a priceless jewel.

"I'll ask around to see if anyone would mind—"

"You're staying here. Argument is over."

She picked up her fork again but didn't take another bite. "You just need to accept the fact that I'm never going to have what you have. But you also need to accept the fact that that's okay. Wherever I end up will be fine. I just need to save some money to replace the fridge that was stolen, as well as all the furniture I'll need to buy."

She'd already had nothing when someone took her stuff. Now she had less than nothing. It was despicable, how a hard-working woman couldn't catch a break. She did everything the way she was supposed to, going to school and getting educated so she could compete in this world. Instead, it put her in so much debt, she practically drowned. If she hadn't sold herself to me, what would she have done?

"I'll keep looking for a place," she said. "But I'll need at least another week before I find something nice that I can afford."

"There's no rush."

"Are you sure?" she asked, tilting her head slightly.

Having her here had been nothing but a pleasure, but that

was exactly the problem. I didn't want to enjoy her company so much. I didn't want to enjoy her body in my bed so often. I didn't want to look forward to seeing her every time I came home from work. "Yes. I'm sure."

———

I WAS SITTING at my desk when Jillian spoke through the intercom.

"Sir? Are you free for a moment?"

I was looking out the window, daydreaming. I turned around and pressed my finger to the button. "What is it?"

"Well, Coen's assistant just called me and told me Coen hasn't been himself all morning. He's locked himself in his office and won't respond to the intercom or anything else. I'm not sure if I should bother you with it, but I wanted to let you know."

If he was having a bad day, why didn't he just go home? Why did he stick around here? "Thanks, Jillian."

"Are you going to go down there?"

"No." I removed my finger from the button then looked at my laptop. I didn't care if my brother was having a bad day. I wouldn't go down there and check on him like some kind of friend. We weren't friends. We were barely brothers. I wasn't sure what we were. Borderline enemies.

My cell phone started to ring. It was Monroe.

She was always pleasant to speak to, so I answered. "Hey, Cherry."

Right from the beginning, her tone was different. It wasn't bubbly and happy like it usually was. "Hey…"

"Something wrong?"

"I'm guessing you haven't seen the news?"

"No. Why?"

She sighed into the phone. "Paparazzi snapped pictures of Simone with some young suit in Central Park. They were holding hands and kissing in broad daylight. She's not even trying to hide it..."

Just like she did with me, Simone had humiliated my brother in front of the entire world. Did she have the class to at least leave her wedding ring at home? Now I knew why my brother was locked up in his office—because he couldn't show his face to the world. He couldn't go home because he shared his space with that whore. "Now it all makes sense..."

"Have you spoken to Coen?"

"No, but my assistant said he's hiding out in his office."

"Are you going to check on him?"

My first instinct was to ignore him and carry on with my life like nothing unusual was happening. I'd warned him this would happen, but he refused to believe me. Why should I feel bad for him? Not only had I warned him, but he also stabbed me in the back. He deserved all of this.

But I still felt bad for him.

"Slate?" Monroe repeated.

"No. I'm not going to check on him. I doubt he wants visitors anyway."

"Slate, this is your brother we're talking about..."

"Yes, I'm aware of the similarity in our DNA. It was exactly the same when he fucked Simone when she was still dating me."

"Now isn't the time to be petty."

"I'm not being petty," I said coldly. "You can't make me care when I don't care."

"But you do care, Slate," she said gently. "I know you do. You're angry at him, but you don't want him to suffer like this. Go down there and be there for him."

"You want me to console him after his wife made an idiot out of him? After she did the same thing to me?"

"I just think you should be a brother to him—regardless of the circumstances."

I was a man torn in two. I wanted to tell him to fuck off, but I also didn't want him ever to experience pain.

"Slate," she pressed. "Go talk to him."

"Why do I always let you boss me around?"

"Because you love my cherry." She hung up.

I set the phone down with a slight smile on my lips, thinking about the woman who set me straight every single day. She was the woman in my bed every single night, the woman who showered with me and listened to me talk about my day. Her stay was supposed to be temporary, but it had turned into a very long sleepover.

I shoved my phone into my pocket and headed downstairs.

———

HIS ASSISTANT TOLD me he wasn't responding to phone calls or knocks on the door. The glass walls surrounding his space had been blacked out with the special technology we used to tint the windows. He could see us—but we couldn't see him.

I moved to the door and tapped my knuckles against the glass.

No response.

I knocked again. "Coen, come on."

Nothing.

I tried the door, but it was locked. "You know this thin glass can't stop me. Unlock it, or I'll break it down." I slid my hands into my pockets as I waited for him to respond to my threat. We both knew I wasn't bluffing. I'd never been the kind of man to unleash empty threats.

He finally turned the knob, and there was an audible click.

I pushed the door open and watched him walk back to his desk. A large bottle of smooth whiskey was sitting on the surface—the top discarded on the floor. There was no glass because he was drinking it straight from the bottle. He fell into the leather chair and got a grip around the neck of the bottle, just as a child held on to a security blanket.

He wouldn't look at me.

I sat in one of the armchairs facing his desk. I crossed my legs and stared at him in silence.

He still refused my look.

My hands rested together in my lap, and I brainstormed my first words. I could be an asshole and say I told you so, but that would make me look like scum. I'd assumed a moment like this would make me feel good, to see karma strike as a form of revenge, but witnessing my brother's sadness changed my tune. All I felt was pity. "I'm sorry, man."

"No, you aren't." He grabbed the bottle and took a drink. "You must have done cartwheels in your office when you heard."

"Have you ever seen me do a cartwheel?" I asked sarcastically.

He drank from his bottle again.

"You gonna offer me some?" I nodded to the bottle in his grip.

"This is all I have—and I'm not sharing."

"Such a gentleman…"

"If you came here to gloat, just go. This is your victory, and you can enjoy it as much as you want—on your own time."

I'd never seen my brother so solemn, so downright depressed. Even when Father died, he wasn't this hopelessly sad. "Coen, I get no enjoyment out of this."

"Bullshit." He finally raised his gaze and looked at me, resembling a ghost. He appeared ethereal, nonexistent. He was just a shadow of the man he used to be—and he still wore his wedding ring. "You warned me about her. You hated me for what I did to you. Then you told me you never wanted to spend another day with me after Mother is gone. So, yes, I know you're enjoying this."

"The only thing I'm enjoying is Simone's absence. Now I never have to deal with her again."

He shook his head. "She owns half of my half. I know she's going to show her face here every single day, crowing about her victory like I have absolutely no feelings." He dragged his hand down his face in self-hatred. "Fuck, I'm so stupid."

"She's not going to do that."

"Trust me, she is. She was after this company from the beginning…and now she got what she wanted."

"You're right, she does want the company. But she'll never have it."

"I didn't sign a prenup, Slate." His eyes moved downward in shame. "She owns half of all my things."

"Actually, you did. You both did."

Coen turned in his chair so he could get a better look at me. With his hand still gripping the bottle, he watched me with pure bewilderment.

"A few weeks ago, we were in the conference room. I told you I commissioned a new destination in Jackson Hole. You two signed off on it. But instead of signing off on that site, you actually signed a prenup that my lawyer drafted for you."

His eyes widened slightly, unable to process what I'd just said. "What?"

"It said she's not entitled to half of your assets, including the company, unless you've been married for at least five years. Pretty standard agreement. You both signed it. I was the witness. It was drafted by my lawyer, so it's concrete."

"But we both didn't know what we were signing."

I shrugged. "Technically. But the judge will rule in our favor—when we pay him off."

Coen finally released the bottle of whiskey he was holding

and sat back in his chair, flabbergasted by the turn of events. "Holy shit…"

"You think I would let that woman ruin your life?" I held his gaze and felt the resentment shoot through my veins. I didn't want to spit on him while he was down, but this moment gave me all the revenge I'd craved. I had his back even when he didn't have mine—and I came out as the hero. My brother would never be able to question my loyalty or goodness ever again. I was the better man—and we both knew it.

Coen stared at me, speechless.

I didn't blame him for having nothing to say. He looked like an ungrateful fool, a man who didn't deserve an older brother like me. Even after he'd betrayed me, I'd still saved his ass—which was more than he could ever say.

He ran his hands down the back of his head as he sighed to himself, overwhelmed by the gesture I'd extended toward him. Then he placed his palms against the desk and looked me in the eye. "So, she gets nothing?"

I nodded. "Not a penny. The evidence of her affair will only drive the nail farther into the coffin."

Coen didn't seem remotely pleased by that. The hurt burned in his eyes like a beacon. All he gave was a slight nod.

"So, what happened? She just woke up this morning and said it was over?"

"In so many words…" He grabbed the bottle and took a drink. "She was very nonchalant about it, like I should have figured everything out from the beginning. She was heartless, cold, and straight to the point. She basically said she got what she wanted and she had no use for me."

What a psychopath. "You really had no idea?"

He shook his head. "I really didn't…"

Sometimes love made a man blind. I just hoped I would never love anyone…because I never wanted to behave so stupidly. I couldn't picture Monroe hurting me like that, but then again, I'd once thought the same thing about Simone. "Since the beginning, she's been after our family money. She wasn't going to stop until she got it—even if that meant robbing the bank."

"I guess so."

"So, she asked for a divorce?"

He nodded. "She didn't waste any time…"

"Because she wants half your money and the continued profits from our hotels."

"Yeah…"

Thank god they were both dumb enough to sign that paperwork. "I have copies and the originals of the prenup. When you meet with your lawyers, just present it. That should be concrete, even if she argues she wasn't aware of what she was signing. You and I will both lie and say she was completely aware of it. Who are they going to believe? A woman who's obviously a gold digger—or us?"

"That would be lying under oath."

I shrugged. "So?"

"You would do that for me?"

It was pathetic he even had to ask. "I don't want that bitch anywhere near this company. I worked too hard to turn it into an empire. I'm not dealing with that psychopath every day. I did this as much for myself as I did it for you."

He stared at me for a long time, speechless again. "I'm sorry I didn't believe you."

His apology meant nothing to me. "I'm just glad this is finally over."

"Yeah…"

We sat together in tense silence, both of us thinking about the blonde who made a fool out of each of us. She made me the laughingstock to the entire world, and now she'd done the same to my brother. Once she learned of the prenup I'd illegally obtained, she would be pissed. So, of course, she would tell the world I was the Cherry Popper, and once again, my name would be dragged through the mud.

Like I gave a shit.

"Did Simone move out?"

"No. She kicked me out."

Wow, my brother needed to grow a pair. "Where are you staying?"

He shrugged. "In this chair."

I shouldn't invite him to my place because I already had a guest, but it felt cold not offering him something. He would never stay with my mother because she would drive him crazy. "You want to stay with me?"

He looked at me like he didn't recognize me. "Seriously?"

I shrugged. "I'm your brother, right?"

"Yeah…but you don't owe me anything."

"I just thought I would ask. You know I have a big place." With multiple floors and multiple bedrooms, it was practically a hotel. "But it's fine if you don't want to."

"No, I would love to stay. Since Simone might take half of everything I own, I'm actually on a budget now."

I would never get married just to avoid that fear. If I met a woman I actually liked someday, she would just have to settle for being my permanent girlfriend. I'd worked too hard to have someone take it all away when they left me. "We won't let that happen, man. We're gonna take Simone down —for good."

———

THE DOORS OPENED, and I stepped inside my apartment.

Monroe was already there, wearing her workout clothes because she'd just finished in my private gym. In her skintight leggings and sports bra, she looked absolutely fuckable. My brother would definitely have to stay on a different floor so he wouldn't have to overhear all the dirty shit I did to her.

She lifted a bottle of water to her lips and took a drink. "So...bad day, huh?"

"No. Good day, actually."

"Am I missing something?"

I stopped in front of her and kissed her on the mouth, liking the way her hair was slightly loose from her ponytail. There was still a sheen of sweat on her rack. Whether she was sweaty, soaked in the shower, or perfectly dry in my bed, she looked like a fantasy. "Coen told me Simone kicked him out. Wants a divorce. Didn't bother hiding the truth."

"And isn't that bad?"

I shrugged. "I knew this was going to happen, so we may as well get it over with."

"And your brother's public humiliation...?"

"A hard lesson that he needed to learn."

"I guess. I still wouldn't call it a good day."

"Well, I actually had both of them sign a prenup without their knowledge. It protects all of Coen's assets, including the company. She'll try to fight it in court, but she won't win, not when we can pay off the judge."

"What?" She put the cap back on the bottle and set it on the counter. "How did you manage that?"

"I lied and said they were signing off on a new property. They were both too stupid to read it."

Her eyes widened. "That's brilliant. But...I don't see how it's valid."

"Coen and I will lie and say she knew what she was signing. She'll fight it, but who is the judge going to believe? An obvious gold digger who publicly betrayed my brother a week after they got married? Or a hardworking man who got run over by a bulldozer?"

"I see your point. Does she know?"

I shook my head. "Not sure. Coen may have told her by now. I wish I could see her face." I smiled at the thought, loving the idea of ruining her stupid little plan.

"I do too." She crossed her arms over her chest and looked at me with new eyes, brilliant gems with luscious eyelashes. The corner of her mouth was raised in a smile, like a thought was making her beam. "So, you've had your brother's back the entire time..."

At the time, I knew Coen was brainwashed and acting stupid. He wouldn't press for a prenup because Simone wouldn't allow it, and he gave her the wheel to his destruction. He was too wrapped up in her manipulative lies to see the truth.

But I was his older brother—and it was my job to protect him.

She kept smiling at me.

"I was just protecting my own ass, alright? If she got part of our company—"

"You are such a liar," she said with a laugh. "You love Coen despite everything he did to you. You're a good man...a really good man."

It was a reputation I didn't want or deserve. "Let's not get carried away..."

"No. Let's." She moved into me and kissed me on the cheek. "I like this side of you."

"I don't. Now let's drop it."

"Impossible." She moved her hands up my chest as she looked at me fondly. "You've been patient with me. You've helped me when it wasn't your problem. And now you've helped your brother even though he did something unforgivable to you. I know Simone and Coen hurt you and turned you into this cold, heartless man. But the real you is still in there."

I sighed as I looked at her, refusing to admit to the possibility she may be right. I'd been burned badly by my own brother. Torched, actually. And I'd never really gotten over it. Seeing the way Simone used my brother only made me more distrustful. But I guess I had a little humanity left inside me.

"Did it feel good?" she asked. "To be right?"

"I always knew I was right, so I didn't feel any different. I thought I might gloat or put my brother down, but when I saw how upset he was, I didn't have a vindictive bone in my body. I think he deserves this, but I don't actually enjoy watching it unfold."

"Because you're a good person."

"Or maybe because I know exactly how it feels…" It was just empathy. My brother was living through the same heartache and humiliation. I'd never loved the woman or married her, but her betrayal cut me to the bone.

"Maybe," she said. "But at least it's over now. You never have to be around her again. You and Coen can be close again."

"That's not gonna happen." I stepped back and felt her hands fall from my body. "I feel protective of him because he's my brother. I don't want him to suffer—even if he deserves it. But I can't see us being close ever again. He still betrayed me—and I'll never forgive him." My brother had never actually apologized for it. I expected him to do it in his office, but the words didn't leave his lips.

Monroe gave me a look of pity but didn't press me on it.

"By the way, he's staying here until he gets back on his feet."

"He is?" she asked in surprise. "He'll be living with you?"

"Yeah. He'll take one of the bedrooms upstairs. There's a small kitchen up there, so he'll have his own space, and we'll have ours."

"What happened to his apartment?"

"Simone kept it."

She rolled her eyes. "Pussy."

I grinned at her choice of words. "I thought the same thing."

"When the divorce proceedings begin, he better grow a

pair and be aggressive. He better not soften when he sees her pretty face."

"I'll remind him."

"You guys are so different, it's hard to believe you're brothers."

"He's not as smart as I am." When Simone dug her claws into me, I got rid of her. But Coen hadn't been so wise. He let her destroy him—handed her the knife.

"Apparently. That's nice of you to let him stay here. I'm surprised he didn't just crash at your hotel."

"Paparazzi will follow him there. My building is a lot more private."

"I guess that makes sense."

"Do you mind if he stays here?"

She gave me an incredulous look. "This is your place. You don't have to ask me."

My eyes moved up and down her body again, loving the way the spandex fit her curves so perfectly. Her hourglass frame was so sexy. My hands ached to grip her tits and squeeze them until she winced. I wouldn't be able to fuck her in the living room or on the kitchen table anymore, not while my brother shared our space. Now I would have to keep it confined to our bedroom—and that's exactly where I wanted to go now.

But then the elevator beeped.

"That must be him," Monroe said.

"Yep." Our fucking would have to wait until he got settled in.

"Once Simone knows what you did, she's probably going to go public with the truth about you."

The thought had slipped my mind. Simone probably would tell the entire world about my fetish, and once the press dug into me a bit, they would realize it was true. That I didn't just pay for sex one time—but hundreds of times. It was a form of prostitution, practically an institution, and I could easily go to jail for it. "Yeah. Probably."

"What are we going to do?"

"Nothing will happen to you. It was a one-time offense. You'll just have to pay a fine."

"And you?" she asked.

"I'll probably have to go to jail."

Her mouth dropped open. "Are you serious?"

"But I could pay off the right people and avoid it altogether. Let's not worry about that now."

"Kinda hard not to…"

My arm circled her waist, and I pressed a kiss to her hairline. "Even if she goes public, the cops will probably look the other way."

"Why would they? You're breaking the law."

"Because I'm their biggest donor. My contributions make up the majority of their funding. Without me, widows wouldn't be taken care of, kids wouldn't have scholarships… the list goes on. It's in their best interest to keep me out of jail —even if I am guilty."

"Is that why you donate to their organization? Just in case something like this happened?"

I walked to the elevator and watched the button light up when Coen reached our floor. "Yes." I didn't do it out of the goodness of my heart. I did it for insurance—just in case one of my girls turned on me.

Monroe didn't look pleased with that information.

The doors opened and Coen was revealed, holding a collection of suits on hangers with a bag at his side.

Monroe smiled as she greeted him. "Nice to see you again, Coen. Let me get your bag."

I grabbed her arm and pulled her back. "No." I pulled the bag off his shoulder and placed it over mine. "Come in, Coen."

My brother stepped inside, five suits on hangers to get him through the week. "Hey, Monroe."

"Did you see Simone?" I asked, assuming he'd gotten all this stuff from his apartment.

"No. The maid gave everything to me. She wouldn't even let me come inside." Even though his assets were secured, he still looked grief-stricken. Even though the entire thing had been a scam, he loved Simone, so the wound was still fresh and festering.

"Bitch," Monroe whispered under his breath.

"No," Coen said. "It's pretty clear I'm the bitch."

I smiled at the self-loathing. "So she doesn't know about the prenup."

"Not yet. I'm excited to see her face when I tell her."

"That makes two of us." Now that she'd shown her true colors, there was no going back. She'd put in the last five years for this reward—but now she wouldn't be getting a cent. "You'll be upstairs. I'll show you." I took him up the stairs to the second floor. There was another living room, a piano, a small kitchen, and a few bedrooms. I took him to a master bedroom and set his bag on the bed. "The kitchen is stocked, so help yourself to whatever you want."

"Thanks." He hung up the suits in the closet then sat on the edge of the bed. With dullness in his eyes and pain in his expression, he seemed numb to everything around him. His hands came together between his knees, and he looked eternally pained.

I didn't know what to say to make him feel better. There were no words to heal a heart broken as much as his. "We're downstairs if you need anything."

"Would you like to join us for dinner?" Monroe offered.

He stared straight ahead and ignored us both. "I'm not hungry. But thank you anyway."

———

I DIDN'T SEE Coen for the rest of the night. We went to bed a few hours after dinner and lay together in the darkness, enjoying our privacy but always aware there was someone else in the penthouse.

She snuggled into my side and rested her head on my chest, her hair cascading across my warm skin. Everything about her was soft, from her strands of hair to her petal-like skin. She always smelled like her perfume first thing in the morning, but as the day wore on, she started to smell like me.

I'd been eager for sex all day, but now that we were alone together, my thoughts kept drifting elsewhere. I knew the situation with Simone wasn't over. She was willing to do anything to get Coen's wealth, so what would she do when everything backfired in her face? She wouldn't go down without a fight. She couldn't be angry at Coen because he'd been too stupid to fight back. I was the one who'd thwarted her genius plan, so she would come after me with a vengeance.

But I wasn't afraid.

She would be a pain in the ass, but I wouldn't let her control my life. She could tell the world I paid for sex, virgins specifically, and perhaps that would ruin my reputation forever. But anyone could make a comeback from anything, and I would do the same.

I just hoped Monroe didn't get dragged into it.

"I can tell you're stressed." Her hand moved over my beating heart.

"Not stressed. Just annoyed."

"Because of Simone?"

I nodded. "I have a feeling the road ahead will be treacherous."

"But the road will eventually reach a dead end—and it'll be over."

"Yes...true." Once Simone told the world the truth, she would have nothing else to fight with. She would eventually have to give up and move on with her life. If I had to take a leave of absence from the company and work from home, that would be fine. I had everything I needed here anyway.

She rubbed her hand against my chest then climbed on top of my body. "Well, I'm not stressed…and I'm not fulfilled either." She straddled my hips and pressed her hands against my shoulders.

"Then let me fulfill you." My hand moved between her legs, and I rubbed her clit the way she liked, in circles with intense pressure. The second we were connected, her hips thrust forward and she moaned at the sensual contact. My fingers slipped inside her and felt the moisture that had already accumulated long before I touched her. She must have lain in the dark waiting for me to get on top of her. When I didn't, she took matters into her own hands.

That was sexy.

My cock was hard in just a few seconds, so I pressed my head against her entrance then dragged her hips back, guiding her down my length until she had all of me. She sat right on my lap, breathing hard as she felt every single inch of my dick deep inside her. She tensed noticeably, like the entire thing hurt her but she wasn't going to complain.

"You want me on top, Cherry?" I liked watching her ride my dick nice and slow, but I knew she liked lying there while I did all the work. I didn't care if she wanted to be lazy or selfish because fucking her was the most enjoyable experience of my life. I would gladly work up a sweat to fuck her.

"I get a choice?"

"Always." My hands palmed her nice tits and squeezed them hard. "You want me on top of you? You want me to fuck you the way you like?"

She gripped my wrists as I fondled her tits. "Please." She rocked her hips back and forth, moving me while I was inside her tight cunt.

I rolled her to her back and pinned her legs back with my arms. I was already buried deep inside her, sheathed by her soaking arousal and profound tightness. I could stay still and enjoy it all night, just the feeling of her incredible cunt. Every time I fucked her, it still felt like the first time, as if she were a sexy virgin who needed to be stretched. I held my face above hers, her beautiful body contorted into the perfect position for me to fuck her. With her knees tucked into her waist and her sexy tits in my face, she was the sexiest woman I'd ever taken. I'd never fucked the same woman so many times. Even with Simone, I wasn't as sexually awake. Monroe was the only woman who made me feel like a teenager, like every screw simply wasn't enough. "I'm gonna fuck you hard, Cherry." I pressed my forehead against hers and made good on my word.

My hips bucked, and I pushed hard and fast right from the beginning. I rammed my dick inside her like she could handle it, like she was a whore who did this for a living. Her moans turned to screams, and that spurred me on even more.

She held on to my arms as an anchor and rocked with my movements, her tits flying toward her chin and then back again. She was living with me for the foreseeable future, rent-free and with access to anything she wanted, but she was paying for it every night by doing this, by letting me be the only man who got to enjoy her.

She always made the sexiest expressions when she came, when her eyes suddenly looked blank like she was staring into the heavens. Then she bit her bottom lip like she was trying to stay quiet even though no one could hear us.

I watched her performance and felt my dick explode inside her. Like a volcanic eruption, I felt the lava in my veins before the big explosion out of my dick. I came inside her with a groan, giving her all of my seed like I did every other day. I filled her completely so she would have it with her all day at work the following afternoon. Maybe when she ate lunch, she would feel the weight right between her legs as it dripped into her thong.

I kept thrusting even though I was finished, feeling my own come move past my length as I rocked back and forth. When the high finally seeped from my veins, I looked down at the woman who slept in my bed every night, the innocent virgin who had become my biggest obsession. "Fulfilled?" I started to pull out of her so I could clean up and go to sleep.

Her nails dug into my arms, and she pulled me back. "Not quite…"

6

Monroe

I WAS RELIEVED SIMONE WAS OUT OF THE PICTURE, BUT I also pitied Coen at the same time. My interactions with Coen had been limited, but it was obvious in that short amount of time that he was heartbroken and humiliated.

Couldn't blame him.

But I was proud of Slate for being the bigger man and supporting his brother. He could turn his back and ignore his brother's pain, but he didn't. He hid his heart deep inside his chest, but he still extended that olive branch. He protected his younger brother then picked up the pieces of his broken heart. What Coen did to his own brother was unforgivable, but Slate was still there anyway.

It made me look at Slate in a brand-new way.

I always knew he had a heart underneath that slab of stone. He paid me for sex, but he also took care of me. He was my rock when everything else fell apart. When someone stole all my possessions, he came to the rescue. He wasn't just the man I was sleeping with, he was also my friend.

I still hadn't found a new place to live because Slate vetoed everything I picked out. He always said the neighbor-hood wasn't nice enough and I needed to move closer to

Midtown, but he didn't seem to understand that I had a tiny budget. Unless I lived with five women in a two-bedroom apartment, there was no way I could live five minutes from my office.

When I came home from work, I walked in the door to see Coen on the other side. He was dressed in a black suit and tie like he'd just left the office. He'd been scrolling through his phone when I joined him. He slipped it into his pocket then looked at me, hollowness in his eyes. His wedding ring was still on his left hand—and that was the saddest part of all. "Hey, Coen. How was work?"

"It was alright." He tried to give a slight smile, but it looked like a grimace instead. "My mother has been blowing up my phone constantly, but I'm not ready to face her yet."

"She's not going to put you down, Coen." Elizabeth would never do such a thing. She didn't like Simone, but she wouldn't let Coen feel stupid for the idiotic decision he made. She would comfort him—the way Slate did.

"Still…I don't want to deal with her disappointment."

"No offense, but they were already disappointed when you married her. Now they'll just be relieved."

The corner of his mouth rose in an insincere smile. "I guess you're right. I made an idiot out of myself in front of the whole world—and I embarrassed my own family. I wish I could take it back…"

"You didn't embarrass your family. They just want you to be happy—with the right person." I hung up my satchel by the door and came farther into the room. I crossed my arms over my chest and looked at the man who seemed so similar to his brother. They had the same facial structure, the same eyes, and the same standoffish attitude.

He looked away, considering what he would say next. "Do you live here?"

"Temporarily. I'm changing apartments right now."

He nodded slowly. "I was hoping you guys were living

together. My brother hasn't had a relationship with anyone in…forever."

"Yes…he's very picky." And he didn't even have a relationship with me. There was this invisible shadow of distance between us, something Slate needed to feel secure. But that distance wasn't really there, not when we spent all of our free time together. He wanted me to get an apartment, but I thought that was only because he enjoyed having me around too much. He felt something for me—but he was still scared.

"He's just been hurt…" Coen didn't admit he was the culprit of that pain, but the guilty look on his face was admission enough.

I wondered if Simone had told him about Slate's cherry fetish. I suspected she didn't because Coen probably would have mentioned it by now. "I know he has. He has a pretty cold exterior, but his heart is alive and well. He wouldn't be so good to you if he really didn't believe in love anymore."

He continued to wear that guilty expression like it was a part of his permanent facial features. It'd been there since he came to the apartment, and it didn't seem like it was disappearing anytime soon. "Does he love you?"

That was a personal question. "We haven't been seeing each other very long…"

"It's been a few months, right?"

"Almost two."

"And you're living with him."

"That's only because I'm in the middle of moving."

He nodded slightly. "Well, he seems really happy with you."

"And I'm happy with him…"

"I haven't even seen my brother with someone in…" He shook his head again. "I don't think I ever have, actually." He stripped off his jacket then hung it over his arm. He wasn't as thick as Slate, but he was built with solid muscle. He had good looks and a nice smile, and it was a shame Simone hadn't appreciated him.

Hadn't appreciated either one of them.

"Your brother isn't really a monogamous guy."

"He is with you."

If only he understood why.

"I can tell you're nothing like Simone. I can tell you like my brother for him."

I did like Slate for who he was, but I didn't know how Coen could have figured that out.

He answered my unspoken question. "Simone truly opened my eyes to reality. Now I see all the warning signs I ignored. And I see a real relationship between two people who actually trust and respect each other. Simone and I never had that. I was just a stepping stone on her way to the lottery." He tossed his coat on the couch with a sigh. "The worst part is, Slate tried to warn me, and I accused him of being jealous of Simone..." He rolled his eyes. "I was such a douchebag." He took a seat on one of the couches.

"Yeah...you kinda were."

The corner of his mouth rose in a smile, and this time, it was genuine. He released a quiet chuckle under his breath. "I deserved that."

I took the seat beside him.

"You know, the only reason I agreed to stay here is to spend some time with him. I could stay at the hotel or rent a place somewhere else. But I thought I could use the opportunity to talk to him. We haven't really talked...in a long time."

It was nice to know he did still care for his brother. "Why didn't you try to be close to him when you were with Simone?"

He brought his hands together as he considered his response. "It was just so awkward when everything came out. Slate was pissed off and wouldn't talk to me. I kept trying to make amends, but he refused to see me. I eventually gave up, and we continued this tense existence that we have to this day. Simone told me he never treated her right and he used to talk shit about me... I should have known that was a lie."

"Slate would never treat a woman poorly. And I think he's proven his loyalty to you...a million times over."

"I know he has. The question is...will he forgive me?" He turned to me like he expected me to give an answer.

"I really don't know, Coen. Even after all these years, it still bothers him. Your betrayal has haunted him for a long time...in a way I can't share with you. It shook his entire foundation, his belief in people and relationships. Even now when I'm with him, I still feel his hollow shell because he tries so hard not to feel anything. He's constantly trying to keep his walls up, even after a few come falling down. Then he builds them back up again."

He rubbed his hands together as he stared at them. "Maybe it's impossible to come back from that."

"Maybe. But he did protect you. He had your back when you weren't even watching. The only reason he would do that is because he still loves you...no other explanation."

"Maybe he does love me. But that doesn't mean he'll forgive me."

"You have to try, right?"

He gave a slight nod. "It just feels hollow, like I'm only doing it because it didn't work out with Simone."

"That's exactly why you're doing it," I snapped. "Because Slate has been right about the entire thing. But maybe Slate's heart is big enough to forgive and forget. I've seen his selflessness, and I think he's capable of it."

"Yeah...you might be right." He grabbed his wedding ring on his left hand and fidgeted with it, as if he was contemplating removing it but wasn't quite ready to. "It's crazy to think that our wedding day really was the happiest day of my life...but it was really the biggest lie of my life."

I felt the waves of sadness seep into my pores as they

washed over me. I could feel his pain like it was my own, could feel his sorrow like I was drowning in it. I hardly knew this man, barely said a few words to him, but since he was Slate's brother, I cared about him like a friend. I placed my hand over his wrist and gave him a gentle squeeze. "Bad things always happen to good people...because good people are always the least suspicious. They're incapable of recognizing evil because they know no evil themselves. You were prey, and she was the predator—and she picked you for a reason."

7

Slate

AFTER I FINISHED IN THE GYM, I WALKED INTO THE bedroom and spotted the white lingerie on the bed where I'd asked my maid to leave it.

I was disappointed Monroe hadn't put it on.

I hopped in the shower, put on my sweatpants, and then walked into the living room. Monroe was sitting on the couch in black leggings and a t-shirt, the loungewear she wore while my brother was in the penthouse. Normally, she would just be in one of my t-shirts with her panties underneath, but since our privacy was compromised, she had to be fully clothed. "Why aren't you wearing the lingerie I got for you?"

"Because it's not bedtime." She rose from the couch and walked around to kiss me.

"So, you'll wear it then?"

"Slate, I know how to take a hint." She had to rise onto her tiptoes to give me a kiss, and the action was sexy because she was so petite. "You'll just have to be patient."

I grabbed her arm and gave her a hard squeeze. "You know I'm not a patient man."

"Yes…I'm aware." She smiled before she pulled away. "I made dinner tonight."

"You?" I asked, unable to keep my surprise in check. "Are we having peanut butter and jelly sandwiches?"

"Ha-ha," she said sarcastically. "No. We're having honey garlic shrimp with mixed veggies."

I continued to look at her in disbelief. "How did that happen?"

"Well…"

Coen walked out of the kitchen and set the plates on the table. "I helped her out a little bit."

"Okay, a lot," Monroe said. "He pretty much did all the work, and I just washed the vegetables."

My hand remained on her arm, and I gave her a playful squeeze, finding her fib cute rather than annoying. "That sounds like teamwork to me. And it smells great."

"I tried to get him to make spaghetti, but he said that was banned."

"it is banned," I said. "That's nothing but carbs. The only time you should ever eat that is if you're running a marathon the next day. And spoiler alert—I'm not a runner."

"You're a lifter." She leaned in and lowered her voice. "And a fucker."

"Exactly, Cherry."

We sat down to dinner, my brother sitting diagonally from me while Cherry sat across from me. I stabbed my shrimp and broccoli with my fork and took a bite. "Not bad." I didn't know my brother could cook, but he'd never invited me over to his place for a meal. Cooking wasn't a hobby of his five years ago, so it was must have been something he picked up during his time with Simone.

"Thanks," Coen said. "I only know how to make about a dozen recipes, but they're pretty good."

"That's more than I know," Cherry said with a laugh. "When Slate said I could only make a sandwich, he wasn't kidding."

"Why don't you teach her?" Coen asked before he took a bite.

"Because I would rather fuck her," I said honestly.

Cherry stilled at my grotesque comment.

My brother tried not to smile before he took another bite. "Fair enough."

"Don't be crude," Cherry said as she gave me a glare.

"Just being honest." Why would I want to spend time teaching this woman to cook when I could just cook for her? The only thing I was interested in teaching her was how to fuck. And she'd mastered that pretty quickly. "Talk to Simone today?"

"Actually, our lawyers agreed to a time and place. We're meeting tomorrow."

"Good." We were finally going to get this shitshow rolling. "It's bullshit that she's in your penthouse."

"Well, she won't be for long," Coen said. "Pretty soon, she'll be trespassing."

"And then she'll be gone for good..." I couldn't wait until the dust settled and this was just a bad memory. "Mother told me she's trying to get a hold of you."

He turned his gaze to his food. "Yeah...I'll call her back eventually."

"What are you afraid of?" I asked. "You already knew she didn't like Simone. It's not like she's going to say anything new."

He picked at his food but didn't take a bite. "I know I disappointed her. I just don't want to see that disappointment reflected back at me. Even if she doesn't say it, I'll feel it. You know?"

I did know, but that wasn't an excuse. "The hard part is just beginning, Coen. You're going to have to stop being a coward and grow a spine. A real man owns up to his mistakes and admits he's wrong. He doesn't dodge his mother's phone calls because he's a pussy."

Cherry gave me a cold look. "Slate…"

"No, he's right," Coen said. "He's always been right."

I didn't mean to kick him while he was down, but his constant fear of conflict was getting on my last nerve. He ran from his problems rather than facing them head on. And sometimes he ignored his problems until he convinced himself they didn't exist in the first place. That was exactly how he got into this trouble in the first place. "You need to call her today or tomorrow. Or I'll call her and throw the phone at you."

He washed down his dinner with a glass of water. "I'll take care of it."

I didn't press him on it.

Cherry finished her dinner before either one of us did. She never ate that fast, but this time, she swallowed her food like she'd been starving. She carried her empty plate to the sink in the kitchen then returned to the table. "I'm pretty tired, so I'm going to bed early. Good night." She gripped both of my shoulders and gave them a quick massage before she leaned down and kissed me on the cheek.

I knew she wasn't tired. She was just pulling this stunt so Coen and I could be alone together. But I let her get away with her plan because I wouldn't call her out in front of my brother. "Goodnight, Cherry."

She left the dining room and disappeared down the hallway.

"That's an interesting nickname," Coen noted.

"It's a lot better than Satanic Whore." I'd never heard Coen call Simone that, but it seemed like the only reasonable nickname for her.

He didn't take the jab offensively. "I like her a lot, Slate."

He hardly knew her. "She's easy to like."

"I'm serious. Simone hated her, so I can only assume that means Monroe is actually a good person."

It was the first time I'd chuckled that day. "Good point."

"Monroe told me she's living with you. It's temporary, but that's still pretty serious."

"It's not. She was just having issues with her living situation. It's not as serious as it sounds."

Coen kept eating and didn't try to correct me. "You like this girl?"

"Obviously."

"But how *much* do you like her?"

I didn't appreciate all the scrutinizing questions. Just a week ago, we'd been enemies who agreed to never spend time together again once Mother was gone. Now that his wife left him, we were suddenly two peas in a pod. "Don't talk to me like we're friends, Coen. I took you in because you're my brother. That's all."

He held my gaze as he absorbed that cruel truth. After a few seconds, his eyes filled with the pain I'd purposely thrown his way. He looked down at his food as if he were going to take another bite, but then he set down his fork like his appetite had been chased away. "I wasn't trying to pry, man. I just...I'm glad you have someone. It's nice having a woman you really care about. My relationship with Simone ended up being a big, fat mistake, but prior to that, I was very happy. I assumed that's how you felt... That's all."

His words seemed sincere, so I felt guilty for rising to anger so quickly. He had no idea about the true nature of my relationship with Cherry, and since Simone was about to tell the entire world, I thought it made sense to come clean. "My relationship with Monroe isn't what it appears to be."

He lifted his gaze and looked at me again. "It seems like you're a couple that's happy together. But that's incorrect?"

"Yes."

"How is that incorrect?" Our dinner was abandoned, and the only thing we had to share was our conversation.

"Because...I paid for her."

Coen wore the same blank look on his face until that revelation really sank in. Once it seeped into his skin and then to his bones, his eyes narrowed slightly. "She's a prostitute?"

"No. I paid for her virginity."

Coen seemed even more confused by that. He rubbed the back of his neck as his eyebrows furrowed. "And you haven't done that yet…?"

"I did months ago. But I've enjoyed having her around so much that I keep paying her to stay."

"So, she is a prostitute?"

"No."

"A prostitute is someone who has sex for money."

"It's not the same, and you know it." When Monroe was done with me, she wasn't going to run out and find a new client. All of her debt would officially be gone so she could really start over. "She had some serious debt hanging over her head. So she came to me. She wasn't comfortable giving it up right away, so I wined and dined her until she was finally comfortable. Then we did it…but I wasn't ready to let her go. So I made another deal with her…for three months."

"How did she know to come to you?"

I'd never told anyone any of this, except Monroe, but since it was going to be public knowledge very soon, it didn't seem to matter. "I've been doing it for five years. I pay good money to pop a woman's cherry. It's an underground thing."

My brother looked surprised but not judgmental. "So… how many women?"

"About a hundred and fifty a year."

His eyebrows rose. "That's over five hundred women…"

"Yeah, that sounds about right." Now that I admitted the truth out loud, I understood just how repulsive I was. I was a rich asshole who took advantage of cash-strapped women just to get off. I paid them handsomely, but that didn't mean it was right.

Coen struggled to keep a reasonable composure. He was

floored by the knowledge, almost visibly disturbed. "That's…
a lot to take in."

"Monroe is the only woman I've been seeing for a while.
Her apartment got broken in to, and they took all her stuff.
She had nowhere to go, so I'm letting her stay here until she
finds a new place."

"That's nice of you…if she doesn't mean anything
to you."

"I never said she didn't mean anything," I corrected. "I
just meant our relationship isn't romantic."

He crossed his arms over his chest as his eyes focused on
the surface of the table. "I'm surprised you told me that."

"Simone knows. She's going to tell the entire world when
she realizes the trick I pulled on her."

His eyes lifted again. "And you would take the ridicule just
to help me?"

My brother really was stupid. He had a loyal brother who
would do anything for him, and he'd taken it for granted for
five years. "You're my brother, Coen. I always have your back
—even if you don't have mine."

As if I'd stabbed him in the chest, he winced before he
looked at the table again.

"I don't care if Simone tells the world. The cops won't do
anything, and I'll just hide out in my penthouse until the next
news cycle kicks in."

"You basically operated a prostitution ring. That's a pretty
big deal."

"And I give the cops a pretty big donation every year."

He nodded. "Now I understand why you wanted to
donate to the police department in the first place…"

It'd save my ass.

"How much did you pay Monroe?"

"Doesn't matter." I wouldn't share Cherry's financial situation with anyone. "But she was in some serious hot water.
She had massive student loans from her undergraduate

degree and her masters, but on top of that, she had a pretty serious medical bill attached to her name for her mother's cancer treatment."

"Shit…that's too bad."

"I made all of that disappear." I gave her a chance to start over, to have a better life without the bank taking most of her paycheck. She would never have been able to buy a house, let alone a car. Finding a husband might even be difficult, since his name would be attached to nearly a million dollars in debt. "In exchange, I get her."

He rubbed his jawline with his fingertips and sighed quietly. "I guess I would have done the same thing if I were in that much debt. Sex is just sex. It really doesn't mean anything most of the time."

"Yeah…" I hadn't been with one woman in a long time, and the sex with Cherry was much better than it ever was with Simone. Even though I didn't trust anyone, a part of me trusted Cherry. I never expected her to betray me because she seemed too innocent of a person.

"How does Simone know this?"

"No idea. She told Monroe when she threatened her."

"Simone threatened her?"

I raised an eyebrow. "Man, she threatened everyone. You were too pussy-whipped to notice."

"I'll say…"

"Anyway, when you meet her tomorrow, it'll come out."

"I wonder what Mother will think…"

She'd be disappointed, probably disgusted. "Honestly, it's not worse than what you did, so I think she'll let it go."

He winced like I'd punched him in the face. "I guess you're right."

The silence fell over both of us now that the conversation had been exhausted. I saw Coen on a regular basis, but I felt like I didn't know him at all. He was a stranger, someone who'd betrayed me a long time ago. My loyalty to my family made me soft. Father was gone, and I was the eldest in the family. I felt responsible for Coen. Mother had already been through enough, and I didn't want this drama to fall into her lap.

My brother turned his gaze on me, visibly apologetic. "Slate—"

"I don't want to hear it."

He winced again.

"I pity you for what she put you through. I know you're a good guy and you deserve better. But the only reason you're trying to apologize to me is because she left you high and dry —and I was right. It doesn't change the fact that you betrayed me. If she'd never left, I would forever be the recipient of your silence. I would never know your children, and when Mother died, we would never cross paths again. That future would have happened because of *you*." I looked him in the eye. "I was the victim in all of this, the person who had to suffer the humiliation of your betrayal. I had to suffer being in the same room with the woman who took my brother away from me. I never cared that she left. It was never about her. It was always about you, my brother, my blood."

"Slate—"

"You made me into a stranger. You made me your enemy. And that's something I can never forgive you for."

———

WHEN I WALKED into the bedroom, Cherry was sitting up in bed reading a book, and she wore the one-piece white lingerie I'd left on the bed earlier.

I was too livid to appreciate the sight.

She shut the book and placed it on the nightstand. "Conversation didn't go well?"

Clothes dropped to the floor as I prepared for bed. My

jeans were tossed aside, and my t-shirt landed on the armchair. "What makes you say that?"

"Your shoulders are stiff, and you haven't looked at me once."

I pulled back the covers and got into bed beside her. "You know me well."

"Very well."

I turned off the bedside lamp and stared at the ceiling. Her lamp was still on, so the room was dimly lit. A beautiful woman in white lingerie was beside me, but I didn't have a sexual urge anywhere in my body. All I could think about was the scar of betrayal that was still marked over my heart.

She snuggled into my side and tucked her slender leg in between mine. Her hand rested on my chest, and her face rested against my shoulder. "You want to talk about it?"

"No."

"Alright. Goodnight." She moved to her lamp, turned the switch, and then came back to me.

With eyes wide open, I stared at the ceiling and listened to her quiet breathing. I was used to the sound as it lulled me to sleep every night. I'd spent every night alone for the last five years, and despite how big my bed was, I had this woman on top of me like there wasn't plenty of space on her side.

But now I'd gotten used to it.

Used to her smell on my sheets. Used to the quiet noises she made in the middle of the night. Used to the way she made the bed every morning even though my maid took care of that.

She didn't pry into my anger and let me be.

But I couldn't get the angry thoughts out of my mind. It seemed like they could only go away after they escaped from my tongue. "I told him the truth about you. Since Simone is going to lose her shit tomorrow, I decided to come clean."

"Oh…"

"He was surprised at first, but then it made sense to him."

"I guess he doesn't have a high opinion of me anymore."

"My brother is a jerk, but not that kind of jerk. He doesn't think less of you. In fact, he told me he would do the exact same thing."

"Well, that's nice." She kept her body wrapped around mine as the lace from her lingerie rubbed against me.

"Then he tried to apologize...but I wouldn't let him."

"Why not?"

"I don't want to hear it. Five years have come and gone, and he never gave a damn. He only cares now because he's been humbled by his humiliation. That's an empty apology, and I'd prefer not to receive that."

"Can't he be humiliated and sincere at the same time?"

"No."

She rubbed my chest with her delicate fingertips. "You were there for him when he didn't deserve it. Maybe that made him realize how much of an ass he has been. Maybe it wasn't necessarily Simone leaving him...but the fact that you were the bigger man. Maybe that's what made him realize he was in the wrong."

"Even if that's true, I don't care." I turned my face toward hers. "And after what he did to me, I don't know why you would want me to forgive him anyway."

"Forgiveness will set you free. Holding a grudge will kill you. At least that's what I've learned in my experience..."

"This man is practically a stranger to me, Cherry. You really think I can just forgive him and forget the last five years?"

"I never said anything about forget."

"I think forgiveness is harder than forgetting." You could block out terrible memories if you really wanted to. But to truly forgive someone for their heinous crimes was too much. For the last five years, I'd had to put up with Coen and Simone at every family event like their relationship was perfectly acceptable. "He didn't apologize to me when it happened. So, it seems ridiculous to apologize now."

"I think you're still very angry and need more time."

"You could give me eternity, and it wouldn't change anything."

"But yet, you protected your brother... That sounds like love to me."

"You can love someone and hate them at the same time." My love for him existed only because our DNA was so similar. There was no other reason. He was my blood, and I had to protect him out of obligation.

"No...I don't think that is possible. I think you want to hate him, but you can't. I think pretending to despise him helps you cope. It's understandable that you need more time. I'm sure Coen can give that to you."

"He can give me all the time in the world. It's not going to change anything."

8

Monroe

SLATE LEFT IN THE MORNING BEFORE I DID.

I filled my thermos with coffee then headed to the elevator doors just as Coen came down the stairs. He was dressed in a designer suit with his satchel over his shoulder. A shiny watch was on his wrist, but his wedding ring was absent.

"Good luck today."

"Thanks," he said, giving me a rueful smile. "I'm sure it'll go terribly."

"Remember, nothing is ever as good or as bad as you think it'll be."

"I'm not sure if that applies in my case." He chuckled slightly then hit the button on the wall.

"Last night didn't go well, huh?"

He shook his head as he slid his hand into his pocket. "No. But I can't blame him for feeling that way. What I did was pretty fucked up, and I never handled it correctly. It just happened so fast at the time. Simone seduced me, fed me lies, and tricked me. She turned me against my own brother like she'd done it a hundred times. She purposely ripped us apart...and I hate myself for allowing that to happen. I believed all of her lies, but seeing how my brother had my back when she stabbed me…made me realize none of that was true."

"I'm sorry it didn't work out."

"Me too." When the doors opened, he stepped inside.

I joined him. "But don't give up on him. I know he'll forgive you. He just needs more time."

"How much time?"

"A lot of time, unfortunately." The doors shut, and we rode the elevator to the bottom floor. "So, he told you about us?"

"Yeah, he mentioned it. I believe what he said, but I don't buy the context."

"What does that mean?" We crossed the lobby together, our shoes tapping against the tile as we made our way through the double doors and to the sidewalk. There were two doormen who always opened the door to residents, day and night. That would be so nice to have at my new apartment, but I would never be able to afford that.

"He says he paid for you. But I see the way you two are together. There's more there than some kind of transaction. He cares about you a lot, more than he will admit. When I saw you two together for the police charity event, I thought my brother was head over heels in love."

"That's just because you haven't seen him with anyone."

"No." He stopped on the sidewalk and gave me a firm look. "I see my brother all the time. I see him when he's angry, annoyed, excited. I've seen him through every emotion under the sun. But with you…the guy is happy. Really happy."

———

AFTER I GOT OFF WORK, I took the train to Brooklyn to check out an apartment listing. It was more expensive than I would usually pay in rent so I knew it was a little nicer than what I was used to, but I was willing to fork over some extra cash so Slate would get off my ass.

It was a one-bedroom apartment with a nice size kitchen, a living room that could fit more than one sofa, and the bedroom had a master bathroom. The neighborhood was decent, and it was really close to the subway station.

It was the best I was going to find.

I called Slate.

He answered before the first ring finished. "Hey, Cherry."

"Hey. Heard anything from Coen?"

"Not yet. I'm sure it's going terrible, though. Simone probably threw a chair out the window."

"I can't see her doing that. I think she would throw the chair at Coen."

He chuckled. "Yes. Unfortunately. Is that why you called?"

"No. Actually, I think I found an apartment. It's really nice, it's in a safe area, and it's affordable."

"Great. What part of Manhattan is it in?"

"Um...Brooklyn."

His silence was filled with combustive anger. "I told you to move to Midtown Manhattan—"

"Just come look at it, alright? You'll see that it's perfectly safe."

"It's two trains away."

"So? I like the train."

"I don't. A weirdo could feel you up on the way."

"That's nothing pepper spray can't fix."

"Are you saying it's happened before?"

I really should keep my mouth shut. "Are you going to come look at it or not?"

"I can already tell you I don't like it."

"Well, I'm getting it anyway, then. It's a great spot, and if I don't snatch it up soon, someone else will."

He growled into the phone. "Cherry—"

"Come look at it. You'll like it."

"No, I won't."

"Then I'm getting it. Bye."

He spoke before I could hang up. "Give me twenty minutes."

I waited outside and scrolled through my phone until he pulled up in his black car twenty minutes later. The back windows were completely tinted so the outside world couldn't make out anyone inside the car. Looking like the president of the world, he stepped out in a navy blue suit and black tie, his jaw cleanly shaven and his eyes hostile.

With my arms crossed over my chest, I watched him walk up to me. "I think you look good in Brooklyn."

His hands moved to my waist, and he kissed me on the sidewalk. "I look good anywhere, Cherry." He squeezed my hips as he kissed me for all the world to see. He pulled me hard against him so I could feel the outline of his dick in his slacks.

"Missed me, huh?"

"I've been thinking about that lingerie I got you all day."

"You could have enjoyed it last night."

"Wasn't in the mood. But I'm definitely in the mood now."

I slipped out of his arms. "Too bad this isn't my apartment yet...we could do it right on the floor."

"I prefer up against the wall."

I took him inside the building and to the apartment I hoped would become mine. "It's been recently remodeled, so it's like no one's lived here. It's got enough space with a nice bathroom. Plus, the neighborhood is good. The subway station is right across the street too."

Slate moved around the room and examined the apartment like a handyman looking for something to fix. He surveyed the kitchen, tested the faucet, and then examined the dishwasher. Then he inspected the locks on the door before checking the windows.

There was no way he could find something bad about the place. I was shocked it was listed at all because anyone would kill to live there. And being right across the street from the subway was an added bonus. I didn't have to walk three blocks anymore. "I told you it was nice." It was an apartment inside a larger building, another luxury I'd never had before. Prior to this, my apartment had always had an exterior entrance.

He came back to me, hostility burning in his eyes. "No."

"No, what?"

"No, you aren't living here."

"What the hell is wrong with it? It's a palace for the kind of budget I'm on."

"There was a stabbing on the corner by the train station just two weeks ago."

"So?" I demanded. "This is New York. There are murderers and rapists everywhere. I could be in Manhattan, and that would still be a problem."

"Well, there are no murderers or rapists in my building."

"But I'm not a billionaire, Slate. I'll never be a billionaire, and that's perfectly fine. This place is good enough for me. I'm always careful."

"I said no."

My hand formed a fist because I wanted to punch him in the face. "You don't tell me what to do. Not now. Not ever."

"I do when I'm paying for you. You're mine for the foreseeable future, and my answer is no." As if he were in a conference room making a pitch, he dominated the conversation with that intense expression that made people shrink back.

"You own my pussy, not me. This is where I want to live."

"You aren't living in Brooklyn."

"There's nothing wrong with Brooklyn."

"It's not Manhattan, and it's too far away from me. What if you need help?"

"I'll call the cops. Slate, I've been on my own for a long time. I don't need you to take care of me."

His intense expression didn't die away. "That's my final answer."

"Fuck you. I'll do it anyway."

"Go ahead. See if they give you the apartment." He turned his back to me and walked to the front door.

"Are you serious right now?"

"Dead serious." He turned around to look at me.

"You can't treat me like a dog, Slate."

"A dog?" He shut the door then came back to me, his powerful shoulders shaking with his rage. "If I were treating you like a dog, I wouldn't give a damn where you ended up. I wouldn't care about your safety. I wouldn't care about taking care of you. On the contrary, I treat you like a fucking queen. You deserve better than this dump. You deserve the best." He stopped in front of me, his eyes still filled with anger even though his words were so gentle. "I'm not letting you settle for anything less."

———

SLATE and I didn't say a word to each other on the drive home. We arrived at his penthouse then stepped into the living room. Coen must have just arrived minutes earlier because he stood there in the suit he'd been wearing that morning.

Slate stepped inside first. "How'd it go?"

Coen set his satchel on the couch then stripped off his coat. "She's bonkers."

"Good." Despite Slate's foul mood, he showed a slight smile. "What did the lawyers say?"

"Mine said it was fully valid. Her lawyer was caught off

guard by it, wasn't exactly sure what to do. She said her signature had been obtained without her consent, but I lied and said she was aware of it. She wanted to kill me, man." He slid his hands into his pockets, partially happy and partially somber. "I've never seen her like that. It felt good...but it hurt at the same time. Our entire relationship was a lie. There's not a single memory that was ever real. And she spent five years waiting for my checkbook. It makes me wonder how many other men she slept with... I got tested today."

"I'm sure you don't have anything, Coen." Simone was the kind of woman who wouldn't allow herself to contract any diseases. She probably fucked lots of different men, but she was safe about it.

He sat on the couch and crossed his legs. "That was just the beginning. Now we have to keep meeting in mediation until we reach a settlement. If we don't, we'll have to take it to a judge for a ruling. Based on her rage, she'll take it that far."

"I'm sure she will." Slate sat in the armchair. "Did she mention my cherry-popper business?"

Coen rubbed his hands together as he stared at them. "No...she didn't."

"Not yet," Slate said. "After she's done being blindsided, it'll be all over the news."

Maybe that was why Slate didn't want me to live so far away from him. If men started harassing me for sex, that could get ugly. I could be stalked or, worse, raped. Maybe that was why he was so anal about it.

"Maybe," Coen said. "Or maybe she'll focus all her fury at me."

"She'll figure out it was me eventually," Slate said. "And honestly, I hope she does. She didn't outsmart me five years ago, and she won't outsmart me now."

Coen bowed his head, as if he were taking the comment personally.

Slate rose to his feet again. "I'm going to hit the gym and

shower. I'll get started on dinner afterward." He left the room and walked into the bedroom.

I stayed behind with Coen. "I'm sorry you had such a miserable day."

"It's not a big deal," he lied. "They always say divorce is a very bloody battle. She was so pissed off when she realized she wasn't entitled to half my estate. That look on her face... I'll never forget it. She was heartbroken...the way I was heartbroken when she left me. Except she's livid over money, and I'm livid over love."

"Yeah...that's gotta be hard."

"It makes it easier in some ways. If she tries to trick me later to sink her claws into my cash, I'll know her apologies are insincere."

"I think your brother might actually kill you if you took her back."

He chuckled. "He'd kill us both."

I scooted to his side and patted him on the thigh. "It'll be alright, Coen. It doesn't seem like it now, but the worst part of your life is officially behind you. Now there's nowhere to go but up."

"I suppose."

"And there are so many women out there who will want you for you."

"I don't know about that part...my reputation is destroyed now. Everyone thinks I'm the biggest idiot on the planet."

"Not everyone," I said. "I don't. Your mother doesn't."

"My mother does," he said with a faint laugh. "She's just too nice to say anything."

"Well, I don't."

"I don't see why. I don't deserve your sympathy."

There was no point in kicking someone who was already down. Mistakes were lessons in life, not life sentences. "You shouldn't be so hard on yourself. We all make mistakes."

"Have you ever made a mistake like that?" he asked, turning to me.

"Well...getting involved with Slate is kinda a mistake."

He held my gaze, his eyes narrowing in interest. "In what way?"

"I really like him...really care about him. When I finally gave in and slept with him the first time, he cut me out of his life. He wouldn't take my phone calls or acknowledge my existence. It hurt so much...and I knew it hurt because I'd become so attached to him. He'd become my best friend...the person I trusted most. And then he offered me more money to stay with him. I wanted to turn it down because I would only get sucked in further, but I couldn't resist. Now I've fallen deeper for a man who won't want me when this is all over. So that's a big mistake, a mistake that will hurt for a long time." I wasn't sure why I'd bared my soul to Coen when I didn't know him well. I saw a damaged individual who needed companionship, and being real with him seemed to heal us both.

"You love my brother."

"I didn't say that..."

"You don't need to."

I cut eye contact because I didn't want to face the truth, not when his eyes looked identical to Slate's. "He's probably going to hurt me so much that I'll never recover. But I'm still here...making it worse with every passing day. If you're an idiot, so am I."

He patted me on the thigh before he pulled his hand away. "You've been so good to me. Why is that?"

"Because you're his brother. When I look at your face, I see him. It's hard for me not to like you."

"Even after what I did to him?" he whispered.

I thought it was wrong on so many levels, borderline unforgivable. But seeing him in this kind of pain erased my anger. "You've been punished enough, Coen."

———

SLATE and I didn't talk until we were in his bedroom after dinner. The last time we'd spoken to each other in private, we were fighting about the apartment I wasn't allowed to rent. It'd been tense ever since.

But it didn't seem like Slate wanted to revisit the conversation. All he did was drop his clothes and get on top of me. Without a kiss or foreplay, he widened my legs and moved on top of me.

"Um, do you mind?" I pressed my palm against his chest.

"Does it look like I mind?" He licked his palm then wrapped it around his tip before he sank himself into my entrance.

"Maybe a kiss to start?"

"I don't kiss when I'm pissed. I fuck when I'm pissed." He shoved himself inside me with a harsh thrust, pushing between my tight walls and forcing me to open, like an apparatus at the gyno. He rammed me right off the bat, making me tap my head against the headboard.

I wanted to protest, but it'd been days since our last fuck, and I didn't realize how much I'd missed it until he was inside of me. I'd been having an orgasm on a daily basis, and the moment that routine was disturbed, I became unhappy. "I think I like it when you're pissed."

He thrust with his arms pinned behind my knees, his cock sliding through the wetness my body secreted the second he was detected. His muscular body tightened and relaxed with his movements, and his large mass blocked out the light from the bathroom and closet because he was so large. He pinned my legs next to my chest and kept going. "I can tell, Cherry."

9

Slate

I WAS SITTING IN MY OFFICE WHEN THE HURRICANE HIT.

Simone marched past the front desk with murder in her eyes. A folder was in her hand, but it may as well have been a gun with that furious expression. Jillian chased behind her. "You aren't supposed to go back there!" She grabbed Simone by the wrist.

Simone was capable of anything, so I hopped out of my seat and moved through the door. "Jillian, it's fine. Go back to your desk." I had a gun in my desk drawer, so if Simone really wanted to take me out, she'd better have a quick draw.

Jillian looked relieved before she headed back to her desk.

I kept the door open for Simone, treating her like a lady even though she was the devil. "I thought you would turn up here eventually."

She threw the folder down on my desk. "What the fuck is this? You fucking piece of shit." She slammed her hand on my desk hard enough to make the solid piece of wood shake. Anger wasn't a good color on her, not when it made the vein in her forehead protrude out like that and the spit fly from her mouth.

Couldn't believe I ever fucked her. "Shouldn't I be saying

that to you?" I returned to my chair and kept my hands in my lap so she couldn't see where they were. "It's been two weeks since the wedding, and you're already divorcing him? Already fucking someone else? I expected you to keep up the charade a little longer...but you obviously have no shame."

"No shame? At least I don't trick people into signing legal documents."

I would never confirm it, not when she was probably recording me. "I have no idea what you're talking about." I smiled, wanting her to know that was bullshit but I was too smart to incriminate myself.

That only pissed her off even more. "You asshole."

"I'd rather be an asshole than a gold digger. So what are you going to do now? The second that paperwork is signed, you're broke. Wow...I wonder if the poor version of you is nice."

"She's not. She's worse."

I smiled wider. "I look forward to seeing that."

She narrowed her eyes like her head was about to explode in a volcanic eruption. "You aren't going to ruin my life, Slate."

"And you're going to ruin mine?" I asked incredulously. "You already did. In case you've forgotten, you tried this number on me, but I was too smart for your games. And I was too smart for your games with Coen too. Accept your defeat and dig your claws into someone else...unless you're too old to get a man's attention now. I guess you'll have to settle for a much older husband who doesn't mind your age."

She slammed her hands down again. "Fuck you."

"And fuck you, Simone. Get out of my office before I call security."

She straightened and opened the folder. She pulled out a copy of the prenup I'd tricked her into signing. "This won't hold up in front of the judge."

"You think so? I think the judge is gonna see a woman

who tried to divorce her husband the second they returned from their honeymoon. And there's evidence of you being unfaithful during the marriage. Who do you think he's going to side with? An upstanding man who gives generous donations to the city? Or a whore?"

Her eyes narrowed. "We both know I'm not the whore."

I knew she was referring to Cherry.

"And even if this doesn't go my way, I won't be poor. You wanna know why?"

"Not really."

"Because Coen paid me five million dollars to shut my mouth about your cherry-popping ways."

Now it was my turn to narrow my eyes. Even when she stormed into my office unannounced, I didn't lose my cool. But now the blood drained from my face from the bomb she'd dropped on me.

"I'm still gonna get his billions. And now I have millions to help with legal fees. We'll see who comes out on top, asshole."

———

I MARCHED into Coen's office.

"I heard Simone just entered the building. Is that why you're here?"

"She stopped by my office for a little chat." I approached his desk. "We need to get her banned from the company. She shouldn't set foot on the property."

"Since she technically still owns some of it, I can't. Believe me, I tried."

"Shit." So she could walk in here at any moment, and there was nothing we could do about it. Why did my brother have to be such an idiot and marry the bitch?

"What did she say?"

"Accused me of tricking her into signing those papers."

"Did you—"

"No. I'm not stupid. But I gave her a big smile as a fuck-you."

"Good."

"She also said something else."

"What?" He stayed behind his desk, his fingers coming together.

"She said you paid her five million dollars to keep her mouth shut about me."

Coen obviously didn't expect me to find out about that because he immediately looked guilty. His fingers clenched tightly together, and he sighed under his breath.

"Five million dollars? What the hell were you thinking?"

"She wouldn't accept anything less."

"She could use the money in the lawsuit. You know that, right?"

"She told me she was going to destroy your life. Monroe's too. I couldn't let that happen. I don't want to give her a dime either, but if that's what it takes to keep her mouth shut, then fine. I wasn't going to let her fuck with you. Sorry...but I'm not sorry."

I didn't want Simone to have any of our money as a matter of pride. But I didn't want Cherry to be harassed for the next few years since everyone would think she was an actual prostitute. I could handle the gossip and the name-calling, but I was a man in different circumstances. Cherry had nothing, and the last thing I wanted was for someone to take something else away from her. "Well...thanks. I can split—"

"No." He lowered his hands and put his feet on the desk. "Simone wants to go to court, which doesn't surprise me. So we'll see how that goes. She'll pull any stunt to get what she wants. I'm prepared to fight just as hard." He rested back against the leather of his chair and brought his hands together on his lap, his fingers interlocked. He seemed to change the subject on purpose, like he didn't want any attention for the gesture he'd made.

It meant a lot to me that he had my back, that he looked out for my self-interest even though he was going through a hard time. "You have a much stronger case than she does. Even if she uses that cash for a good lawyer, it won't give her a good chance. And we can give the judge a yacht for his troubles, something the Feds can't trace."

"I never use my yacht anyway. I'm sure Simone would get much better use out of it...but I'd rather sink it than give it to her."

Simone was the nightmare that haunted my dreams, but instead of getting angry about it, I had to remind myself she would be gone soon. My brother would get the better deal out of the settlement, and then she would be gone for good. I'd never exercised so much patience in my life.

"Monroe has been exceptionally nice to me...considering Simone threatened her."

"You aren't Simone."

"But still...she's a good woman."

A very good woman. A strong but innocent woman. She brought out the best in me because she beat out the worst. "She is."

He stared at me for a long time, meaning lingering in his eyes.

"What?"

"I've been with a manipulative bitch for the last five years. Now that I've come out of the fog, I see so fucking clearly. I see a woman who never gave a damn about me. Because of that, I see Monroe in a new way. I see the kind of woman I wish Simone had been. I see someone honest, caring, and self-less. You're really going to let a woman like that go?"

"Who said anything about letting her go?"

"You're still acting like it's a transaction. Sounds like the same thing to me."

I knew my brother was trying to help me, but we weren't close enough for this kind of conversation. "Stay out of my personal life, alright?"

"I'm just looking out for you. Monroe mentioned you dropped her the second you got what you wanted last time. Don't make the same mistake."

Now I liked this even less. "Don't talk to her about my personal life either."

"I'm just trying to help."

"Well, don't," I snapped.

My brother kept up the same expression, like he knew something I didn't. "Even though Simone turned out to be the biggest mistake of my life, I really liked being in a relationship. I liked coming home to the same person every day, sharing my life with them, and just being together. One-night stands used to be my thing, but they got old after a while."

I rolled my eyes. "Cut the shit, man."

"I'm being serious. You only turned to cherry popping because of me and Simone. I'm sorry for that...I really am. But I think it's time you put the past behind you and try again, this time with the right person. Monroe isn't Simone... she'll never be Simone."

"You think I don't know that?"

He shrugged. "I don't know...do you?"

I'd had enough of this conversation. "I'll see you at home later."

"Alright...but think about what I said."

———

WHEN I GOT OFF WORK, I met with my real estate agent. She took me to a quaint townhouse just a few blocks from where I lived. It was right off the sidewalk in a nice neighborhood, close to the park and on the upside of town.

She took me inside and showed me the 2,000-square-foot

home with the full kitchen, living room, and several bedrooms. It was a little big for a single person, but Monroe wanted a husband and a family someday. It would be perfect for that.

Then she would have everything she needed.

No debt. A good job. And a nice place to live.

I wouldn't have to worry about her again.

The agent followed me until we returned to the entryway. "It's not officially on the market yet. If it were, it would already be gone. But I wanted you to have the first opportunity if you wanted it."

"I'll take it." I could picture Cherry growing old in this place, raising a family and then watching her kids leave for college. I could picture her and her husband watching TV after making dinner in the kitchen. The thought made me happy, but also sad at the same time. While she was living her dream, what would I be doing?

Would I be a fifty-year-old man still popping cherries?

Would I be rich and alone?

Would my only legacy be my brother's kids?

"How did you want to do this?" she asked. "In cash?"

"Yeah. In cash."

———

I SHOWERED after I hit the gym and then stepped into the living room.

Coen was there nearly all the time now. In the beginning, he stayed upstairs and thrived in his own space, but now he felt comfortable enough spending his evenings with us. Right now, he and Cherry were playing a card game at the kitchen table.

"Ha." Cherry threw her cards down. "I win again."

Coen stuck out his tongue. "You suck."

"At least I'm not a poor sport."

"I'm not a poor sport," he countered. "I just think you're cheating."

"Am not." They bickered back and forth like siblings.

I walked up to the table and rested my hands on the surface. "Coen, could you give us a few minutes? I need to talk to Cherry about something."

"Uh, sure." Coen detected my serious mood and excused himself from the table. "I want a rematch later."

"Sure," Cherry said as he walked away. "I'll kick your ass then too."

I sat across from her and watched her shuffle the deck before she returned the cards to the box. "What's wrong? You're awfully serious."

"I have something to tell you."

"Oh? I'm listening." She folded her hands on top of each other on the surface of the table.

I pulled out the listing I'd printed off and set it in front of her.

She looked down at the townhouse, seeing the picture of the front as well as the images from inside. Her serious expression turned to one of pure bewilderment. She flipped the page then raised her chin to look at me. "What's this about?"

"You said you always wanted to live in a townhouse."

"Yeah, but why are you showing this to me?"

"Because it's just a few blocks from here, it's in Manhattan, and you could walk to work."

She looked at the paper again. "It doesn't show the price, but I can guarantee you that I could never, ever afford this place." She pushed the papers back toward me. "Maybe someday when I invent something and become a millionaire. But until that happens, I'll be a renter for the rest of my life."

I pushed the papers back toward her. "Cherry, I bought it for you."

Her features looked exactly the same, frozen in shock. It took her several seconds to process what I'd said, as if she couldn't believe any part of it. "What did you just say?"

I just gave her the one thing she wanted more than anything, so she probably couldn't believe her luck. It was a dream come true. Before she met me, she had nothing. She struggled every single day of her life. But now I'd wiped away all the terrible things that haunted her. "I bought it for you. It's yours."

The look she gave me was one I didn't expect. Her eyes formed a thin layer of moisture, but it seemed to be from fury rather than touching emotion. She slowly sat back against the chair, like I'd just given her the worst news she'd ever received. She looked down at the papers I'd pushed toward her and then ripped them into pieces.

I watched the shredded pieces fall from her hands and litter the table and floor. When I looked at her again, she seemed even more furious than she was just a second ago. I was meeting the gaze of a woman I didn't know. "Cherry—"

"I don't need you to buy me something, Slate. I'm perfectly happy in an apartment in Brooklyn."

"But—"

"If you really want to keep me safe, you could ask me to move in here with you—permanently. Slate, I don't want your fucking money. The only reason I agreed to this arrangement was so I could be with you a little longer. When will you get that through your damn head?" She tapped her forefinger against her temple. "I don't want you to buy my dream house so I can move out and never see you again." She rose to her feet and brushed the pieces of paper onto the floor. "I don't want your money. I don't want the townhouse. I just want you." She stormed off into the bedroom and slammed the door behind her.

I stayed at the table and listened to the silence once she departed. The shreds of paper were scattered everywhere, and I replayed the conversation we'd just had over and over. I imagined her face lighting up when I presented my generous gift. I never anticipated such painful rage. I never imagined it would hurt her instead of making her happy. Now I didn't know what to do, what to say. So I just sat there, hoping she would come back.

————

AN HOUR LATER, Coen returned downstairs.

He approached the table and looked at the scattered pieces of paper everywhere. He stared at them on the floor before he rested his arm on the back of Cherry's vacated chair. "Did you get a new shredder or something?" He grabbed a few scraps and pieced them together, trying to rebuild what Cherry had destroyed. He kept working until a small fragment of the picture was restored. "Looks like a house."

"I bought Monroe a townhouse." My voice came out emotionless because I was dead inside. My gesture had been turned upside down. She'd used it as a weapon to stab me to death. Now I was bleeding all over my kitchen table.

"Oh…that's nice of you."

"I thought so too."

He helped himself to the chair. "I guess she didn't see it that way?"

I shook my head.

"I told you Monroe was nothing like Simone. She doesn't want your wallet."

No, she certainly didn't. She had a greater chance of getting my cash than my heart, but she still chose my heart. She could have accepted the townhouse and moved on with her life. But instead, she wanted much more.

"I think this is a good thing."

"I disagree."

Coen gave me a disappointed look. "You have a beautiful

woman who wants you for you. I think that's worth more than all the cash in your bank account."

"She knows I'm not interested in something serious."

"But you're already in the middle of something serious. You just have a different label on it."

"I didn't realize how she felt..." I didn't realize how attached she was to me, how she wanted something permanent rather than temporary.

"It's pretty obvious, man. That woman wears her heart on her sleeve—you're just blind."

"I was clear about what I wanted in the beginning."

"Supposedly. But you've been bending the rules ever since. How many townhouses have you bought for your other cherries?"

None.

"How many other cherries have lived with you? Or better yet, stepped foot inside this apartment?"

None.

"She's never been like the others. Why don't you just try to give the woman what she wants?"

"Because I have nothing to give." I rose from the table and left my brother behind. By this time of the evening, we should be eating dinner then getting ready for bed. But the night had been ruined once I gave her that gift.

I walked into the bedroom and found her sitting on the couch in front of the TV. The screen was black, and the darkness of the night filled the bedroom. I turned on a few lamps so it wouldn't be so dark.

She didn't look at me. "I would leave, but I have nowhere to go."

"I don't want you to leave." I sat in the armchair and looked at her stretched out on the sofa. The cashmere blanket was pulled over her shoulder. Her hair was spread out around her, and she looked so petite on the large couch. Everything in my apartment was several sizes bigger, dwarfing her petite body.

"Really? It seems like you want me to run to that townhouse."

"No. I don't even have the keys for it yet."

She kept her eyes away from me, as if she refused to acknowledge my existence.

"Cherry—"

"I'm not sure if I can do this anymore." She pulled herself up and let the blanket fall from her shoulder. There were small bags under her eyes like she'd shed a few tears. "I know you already paid off my loans so I can't reimburse you the money, but...I don't want to be here anymore."

Crueler words had never been spoken to me. That was the most painful sentence ever to come from her mouth. My gift drove her away, and now she wanted nothing to do with me. It hurt more than my brother's betrayal.

"I knew this was going to be a mistake, but I didn't realize how big of a mistake it would turn into. You're such a strong man, but you continue to let the past defeat you. You continue to let Simone's betrayal break you. You've allowed her to ruin your life, even all these years later. You have a woman who actually cares about you, but you refuse to give her a chance... It's pathetic." She crossed her legs and her arms and focused her gaze out the window. "I see myself falling harder for you with every passing day...but I see you growing more distant. When I couldn't find an apartment you liked, I thought it was just an excuse to keep me at your penthouse. But then you went out and bought me my dream home...just to get rid of me."

"I'm not trying to get rid of you. I'm trying to take care of you."

"That's not how I want to be taken care of." She finally turned her gaze on me, her eyes slightly watery. "I want to sleep beside you at night because I know that's the safest place in the world. I want you to take me out to dinner once in a while. I want you to bring me flowers for no reason. That's how I want you to take care of me, not by buying me a fucking house."

I didn't want to be insensitive, but I wondered if her attachment came from the context of our relationship. "I'm the first man you've ever slept with, so I understand why you're attached to me."

She rolled her eyes. "No. Like a normal human being, I actually have feelings for the man I'm sleeping with. There are so many things I admire about you, and there are so many things I despise about you. But at the end of the day, you're still my best friend. At the end of the day, you're still the man I want to come home to every night. It's not because you're the only man I've ever been with. That has nothing to do with it."

If I'd known this would be her reaction to the townhouse, I never would have gone through with it. But I also didn't know what else to do with her. The last thing I wanted was for her to end up in a trashy apartment on the bad side of town. I wanted to know she was safe, whether we were together or not. "I didn't realize you felt that way."

"Because you're an idiot," she jabbed. "It's written all over my face. Even your brother noticed."

Maybe that was why he was pestering me about her so much. "I wasn't trying to offend you, Cherry. I thought that townhouse would make you happy. You said you've always wanted to raise a family there."

"Yes, but the only person I want to raise a family with is you." She looked away as she said that last part. "So why would I need a townhouse? The last thing I want is the magnificent items your wallet can buy. I just want you…"

The silence was so loud, it sounded like a drum. My heartbeat thudded against my chest painfully, like I was about to jump feetfirst into a fistfight. I heard every word she said, and the significance of each one was profound. She didn't tell me she loved me, but she didn't need to. Everything she'd said was a declaration in itself.

I'd been blind to her feelings this entire time.

I remembered exactly how it felt when Simone left me. I remembered how much it hurt. I got over it quickly because she wasn't worth my heartache. But that pain still left a scar on my chest. Now I was hurting Cherry, a woman who only deserved the good things in life. I was Simone in this situation, a soul-sucking leech.

I didn't want to hurt her.

That was the last thing I would ever want.

I brought my hands together and stared at the rug under my feet. When I'd come home that evening, I'd expected to be greeted by Cherry's smile and warmth. I'd expected her to be touched by the gesture I made. Instead, I'd ruined the best thing in my life. Now we were at a dead end, and there was no going forward.

It was over.

"Don't worry about the loan. No hard feelings."

"What's that supposed to mean?" she whispered.

"I'm releasing you from your obligation." I kept my eyes on the rug so I wouldn't have to see the devastation on her face. "You'll stay here until the townhouse is officially ready. Then you'll take the keys and leave."

"I told you I don't want—"

"I already put it under your name. It's done." That was a lie, but I wanted her to have the property anyway. I wanted to know she was taken care of. If not, I would constantly worry about her.

"I can always sell it—"

"It's yours, Monroe. I don't want it. That's final." The endearing nickname I used to use died in my throat. Now I could never call her that again, and that was one of the worst parts of all. "I didn't realize how you felt. I didn't realize you wanted more. That's something I can't give you, so we should end this now before it gets worse."

"You can't be serious…"

"But I am." I lifted my gaze and looked at her, seeing the devastation on her expression that mirrored the pain in my heart. "I can't give you what you want. I refuse to make you feel worse…regardless of how much I want you."

The film in her eyes slowly started to grow.

"I'm sorry…"

"I don't believe you," she whispered. "I know you care about me."

"Of course, I care about you. But I don't want any of the things that you want."

"Or you refuse to allow yourself to want them. Slate, you're happy with me. You care about me. You trust me. It's just been the two of us for months now—no one else. You couldn't let me walk away then, and you shouldn't let me walk away now."

"I have to, Monroe."

The film turned into drops of tears. "Don't let her ruin your life."

"It's not because of her."

"It is because of her. You're too scared to let anyone in. I'm not like her. I'm not like Coen. I would never hurt you. You're the one who keeps inflicting all of the pain."

"And that's why you deserve someone better."

"I don't want someone better," she whispered. "I want you. You've never bent over backward for any other woman. You've never worked so hard to be with someone else. That has to be mean something."

"It means I like the chase."

"Well, you haven't chased me in a long time. I've been here every single night, right by your side. We've fucked on the couch, gone to your brother's wedding, and spent every free moment together. You're going to sit there and tell me that doesn't mean anything?"

"I didn't say it didn't mean anything. It just doesn't mean as much to me."

She turned her face like I'd slapped her on the cheek. "I refuse to believe that."

"I don't care what you believe." When I woke up that morning, I'd rolled her onto her stomach and fucked her from behind before I got ready for my day. I thrust my hips until she came with a scream, and I followed right behind her. But now that felt like a different time. That was the last time I would ever sleep with her. Doing it now would be too painful. "I'll sleep in a different room. You can stay in here."

"This is your bedroom. I'll go." Tears had streaked down her face, so she wiped them away with both palms before she rose. She sniffled loudly before she grabbed her bag from the closet and started to stuff it with the clothes I had bought for her.

All I could do was sit there and deal with the painful tension, the weight of goodbye. I wanted to leave the penthouse altogether and go to my hotel, but that felt cold and cowardly. Watching her leave would be hard, but not saying goodbye would be worse.

She grabbed her things and left the bedroom without a backward glance. This time, she didn't slam the door.

She didn't even close it.

10

Monroe

HIS PENTHOUSE WAS HUGE, SO I HAD NO PROBLEM FINDING a vacant bedroom upstairs. I just picked one at random and found a queen-size bed, two nightstands, a large TV on the wall, and a dresser underneath it. It had its own bathroom, and I wondered if every bedroom in the penthouse had its own bathroom.

Once I was alone, I finally let my tears fall. Before, I did my best to hold them back, but now I couldn't restrain them at all.

I wished I hadn't made such a scene when he gave me that townhouse. It was generous and thoughtful, but it also reminded me that he wanted me to have somewhere to live once he was done with me. I didn't want to live in that beautiful townhouse. I wanted to stay right here, sleeping with that man every single night for the rest of my life.

He didn't feel the same.

I didn't expect him to reciprocate my feelings completely. But I expected him to at least feel something. I expected him to want to take things slow, to see where they went. But he wouldn't even give me that.

He wouldn't give me anything at all.

When I heard a subtle knock on the door, I sucked in a deep breath and stifled my tears, hoping it was Slate with a change of heart.

The door opened, and Coen poked his head inside. He took one look at me before his eyes fell in sympathy. He stepped inside and shut the door behind him. "I thought I heard someone crying in here."

I sat with my legs crossed and a pillow hugged against my chest. "You guessed right."

He stepped into the bathroom and grabbed a few tissues before he handed them to me.

"Thanks…" I wiped away my tears then blew all the snot out of my nose.

He glanced at my bag on the dresser before he correctly guessed what happened. "My brother is the smartest guy I know, but when it comes to this, he's also the dumbest guy I know. Simone made me blind to the truth, and fear made Slate shield his eyes from reality."

I clenched the wet tissue in my hand until I'd rolled up in a little ball. "I tried to talk to him…he didn't feel the same way."

"He says he doesn't feel the same way, but I don't buy that."

"It doesn't matter if he does or doesn't. He's too stubborn and afraid to change his mind."

"Let's hope that's not true." He raised his hand against my back and rubbed it gently, comforting me like he was my own brother. "What now?"

"He bought me a townhouse…"

"And he says you don't mean anything to him…"

"He expected me to be grateful, but I was just pissed off. I don't want a townhouse. I want to stay here with him…"

"And he didn't want the same thing?"

I shook my head. "I told him I didn't want the townhouse, but he insisted on me keeping it. I don't have a lot of options anyway, so I guess I will…but it still hurts."

"Yeah…I can imagine."

"He said he didn't want to hurt me anymore. He released me from my obligation. Now I don't know what to do. I don't want to sleep alone, even in that nice townhouse. I'm so used to sleeping with him that I can't imagine sleeping alone again."

"Yeah, it's difficult to get used to it. I slept beside Simone for five years…now that king bed is all mine."

"I don't want to date someone else either. I was seeing this nice guy named Wyatt when we broke up the first time. He told me to call him if it didn't work out with Slate, but I don't want to do that. This is the only place I want to be. But it doesn't seem like he can let go of the past. It doesn't seem like he can ever trust again."

"You're right. I don't think he can. Not yet anyway."

"I'm afraid it'll be too late when he does trust again." I grabbed another tissue and wiped away the new waterfall of tears. "Because I can't mope around forever. The sorrow will kill me." I blew my nose then grabbed another tissue.

"I'll try to talk to him. I've already tried a few times, but I'll try again."

"Thanks, Coen."

He rubbed my back. "I don't want my brother to lose the best thing that's ever happened to him. He's too scared and stubborn to have a real relationship again, but eventually the sadness will kill his fear. I just hope it doesn't take too long to happen. You're a beautiful, kind, and successful woman. It won't take long for someone to scoop you up."

I couldn't imagine being with anyone else but Slate, but if months passed and I didn't hear from him, I would be forced to move on. I'd already let him break my heart. I couldn't let him own my heart too. The last thing I wanted was to become a hurt and bitter person the way he was, to let the pain fester so much that it infected my future relationships. I learned from his mistakes. I just wished he could learn from them too.

11

Slate

I DIDN'T SLEEP THAT NIGHT.

The only time I closed my eyes was when I blinked.

The sheets smelled like her so it seemed like she was with me, but the coldness on her side of the bed made me realize she wasn't. It was just me in this big bed—entirely alone. She was still in the penthouse, but it seemed like she'd disappeared from the earth.

When I got ready for work, she had already left the penthouse. I stepped into the kitchen to pour a mug of coffee and noticed her thermos was missing, the one she took to work every single day.

I sipped my coffee at the kitchen counter and wiped the exhaustion from my eyes. It hadn't mattered how tired I was, I just couldn't fall asleep. My thoughts kept swirling around that painful conversation that ended with her storming out of the room with tears running down her cheeks.

This was all my fault.

I never should have pursued her in the first place. I should have let Wyatt have her. I should have let her move on from me instead of giving her an offer she couldn't refuse. Now I'd broken her heart when that was the last thing she deserved.

"I know I'm an idiot for marrying Simone, but you're the bigger idiot."

I turned around at my brother's voice.

"I went into her room last night, and she told me what happened." He was dressed in his designer suit and ready for court. The laborious bickering would begin today in front of a judge until a settlement was reached. I had to come in too to make a statement.

"Why were you in her room?" I asked, my nostrils flaring with suspicion.

"Because I heard her crying—because of you. You'd rather I ignore it?"

I sipped my coffee and tried not to be angry with him, not when this was all my fault. I was the only person I should be angry with right now.

"What the hell are you doing? Seriously?"

"Stay out of it."

"No, I won't stay out of it. You told me to get rid of Simone, and I didn't listen to you. Now I need to tell you when you're being a huge idiot. Letting her go is the biggest mistake of your life. I'm telling you..."

"I don't do relationships. Never have and never will."

"You did one relationship." He held up a forefinger. "And it was a terrible relationship. She used you and then seduced your brother to spite us both. Come on, she did a number on both of us, and we're both fucked up because of it. But don't let it ruin what you have with this woman. I'm telling you, another guy is gonna snatch her up so quick..."

"And I can't blame them." The idea of her bringing a guy home from a bar made me jealous—extremely jealous. Seeing her with Wyatt had ripped out my insides. It made me so furious that I marched down there and did whatever I could to get her back. When I saw her with someone new, would I do the exact same thing?

"Slate, come on." He threw his hand down. "She's been

living with you for a while, and she obviously makes you happy."

"Because we're fucking."

"It's more than that, and you know it. You could fuck a different woman every night for free, and you wouldn't need her at all. Monroe is the only woman who's been in your bed in five years because she actually means something to you. You don't have to marry her or profess your undying love for her. But give her something."

"Like I already said, I have nothing to give." I was a grouchy old man in a young person's body. I was bitter like the world hadn't been good to me for many decades. It seemed like I'd lived too many years, seen too many hardships.

"That's bullshit, and you know it. Despite what I did to you, you were still there for me."

"And I've been there for her. I've made all of her problems go away—because I care about her. I bought her that townhouse so I would know she would always be taken care of. That's the extent of my emotions." I took another drink of my coffee before I left the mug in the sink. "What time do you want me there today?"

"We're just going to change the subject now?"

"I'm not changing the subject. Conversation is over. Now, what time?"

"One. And are you sure you want to do this?"

"I want Simone to lose, and I'm willing to do anything to make that happen—including lying under oath."

———

I SIGNED ALL the paperwork at the office and received the keys from the real estate agent. Once the transaction was completed, Monroe officially owned her own piece of property. To the average person, it was an expensive piece of real estate, but to me, it was just pennies. Not only would Monroe have a place to live, but she would always have some wealth in her name. If something terrible happened, she could always sell it for the equity.

I called a designer next and asked them to decorate the space, providing the living room furnishings, bedroom sets, and dining table. Monroe didn't own any furniture, so she would need to get started somehow.

Dread had been sitting in my stomach all afternoon because I didn't want to come face-to-face with Monroe. I didn't want to watch her walk out of my life for the final time. I didn't want to acknowledge that our arrangement was officially over. She'd been the woman in my bed for months, and now my bed would be empty for months. Running out and grabbing tail right away didn't feel right.

And I couldn't go back to my cherry-popper ways. Those days were over.

Monroe's was the last cherry I would ever pop.

When it was almost one, I realized I had to run over to the courthouse a few blocks away. I put the keys to the townhouse on my ring and then had my driver take me to the building where the hearing was taking place.

I joined my brother minutes later. We were in private in the break room, so I spoke freely. "How's it going?"

"I think the judge is leaning toward me. Simone's having a hard time keeping her cool. When we played the video of her and that guy in the park, she nearly lost her shit." He added more coffee to his cup and took a drink. "She's lucky she got the five million from me. I don't think she's getting another cent."

"Good. She better not."

"You're sure you still want to do this? Because you don't have to."

"I know, Coen. And I definitely want to do this." I would be lying under oath, which was a crime, but I was willing to do anything to help my brother get rid of the parasite that had burrowed its claws into his skin.

"Alright. No going back."

"No going back."

"Have you talked to Monroe today?"

I glared. "You really want to talk about her right now?"

"Until you get your head on straight, I always want to talk about her."

We returned to the courtroom where the meeting was being held. Coen had his expansive legal team, and Simone just had a single lawyer along with his assistant. She looked like she wanted to kill me the second I walked into the room.

Revenge was so sweet.

We took our seats, and the judge continued the hearing. Since I was the only witness to the legal documents, he asked me to recount my story.

"The three of us were in the conference room at work. My assistant Jillian had just brought in coffee and snacks. I had the paperwork for the new development we're establishing in Jackson Hole. We signed that first, and then Coen and I asked her to sign the prenup since they were getting married in a week. She signed it." I wasn't a big fan of lying, but I wouldn't hesitate to play dirty when Simone was trying to ruin our lives.

Simone practically growled. "Liar. Fucking liar."

"Silence," the judge commanded. "If you can't control your outbursts, then you can leave."

She turned silent, but her look was still furious.

The judge turned to me. "Is that the truth?"

"Yes." I looked him in the eye.

"And Mrs. Remington knew what she was signing?"

It was a sin that she got to have our last name. It made my insides churn. "Yes. But she didn't look over the paperwork very carefully. However, she knew what she was signing, and it's not our fault she didn't read every line or consult her own lawyer about it. That's her mistake, not ours."

Simone's eyes looked like they were about to burst out of her head.

"And why did you have the paperwork?" the judge asked.

"Coen and I have the same lawyer. I advised him he should get the prenup. He resisted at first, but then he found my reasoning sound. So our lawyer drafted it, and I picked it up on the way to work that day." Coen and I worked out our story many times before we appeared today to make sure our stories matched.

The judge looked over his notes before he looked at me again. "I have no further questions of the witness."

That was my cue to be excused, so I left the room silently, leaving my brother to his fate.

———

WHEN I CAME HOME, the first thing I did was look for Monroe. She was usually home before I was, but I didn't see her in the living room or the kitchen. A conversation sounded painful, but I couldn't avoid her forever. I went upstairs to her new bedroom.

She was lying on her back staring at the ceiling, her hands resting on her stomach like she was about to be placed in a coffin. I tapped my knuckles lightly against the door so she would know I was there.

She sat up quickly. "Coen?" When her eyes settled on me, she looked disappointed.

That hurt in ways I couldn't explain. I came up there to talk to her, but now I didn't have a single thing to say. I was stuck there, put off by her assumption that I was my brother. A flashback of catching Simone with Coen played in my mind.

She didn't seem apologetic for the mistake. "How did court go today?"

She wanted to talk about my brother? "It seems to be going his way."

"Good. That's how it should be." She pulled her knees to her chest and wrapped her arms around her knees. "I talked to one of the girls at work, and she said I could stay with her until I figure out my living arrangements."

"We already figured it out."

"Slate, I really don't—"

"Take it. Even if you don't, it's in your name. It's just going to sit there. You can sell it if you want, but it makes more sense just to live there."

She watched me with eyes pregnant with pain.

"I got the keys today." I dug into my pocket and pulled them out. I detached them from my key ring before I tossed them onto the bed beside her. "I had an interior decorator look at the place and order stuff for you. It'll be there in a few weeks."

She rolled her eyes. "Of course you did..." She didn't reach for the keys.

"You're welcome to stay here until you get a bed. You'll ruin your back sleeping on the floor."

"I'll get an air mattress."

I wasn't surprised she didn't want to stay here, not after the conversation we'd had last night.

"I guess I'll leave, then." She eyed the keys without taking them. "No reason to hang around..."

Our relationship had been built on friendship, and we'd gone from being lovers to being strangers. That connection we used to feel was long gone. Her disappointment was palpable, and her heartbreak so audible, it sounded like shattered glass. Everything we'd built in the last few months was destroyed. "I'm sorry...I never wanted to hurt you." I meant those words from the bottom of my heart.

She looked at me, and the disappointment disappeared for a moment. "I know you didn't, Slate. I just wish you were able to move on from the past, to understand that you can trust me...because not all people are evil."

"I know they aren't."

"And I would never hurt you, Slate."

"I know that too..."

"Then what just makes all of this worse." She got off the bed and grabbed the two silver keys I'd given to her. She felt them in her palm before she shoved them into the pocket of her jeans. With her head down, she grabbed her bag off the dresser and shouldered it. "It's time for me to leave."

I blocked her way to the door, my body making the movement subconsciously. Now that it was time for her to walk out of my life forever, I didn't want to let her go. I didn't want to watch her step inside the elevator and see the doors close for the last time. Even if this was the right thing to do, it didn't make it easy.

She held the bag and looked at me with watery eyes. "I have another bag in the closet. Could you grab it for me?"

I would do anything for her, so I didn't hesitate. "Sure." I walked across the room and opened the white French doors, only to discover there was nothing there. It was completely empty. "Monroe?" I turned around to look at her.

But she was gone.

She left without saying goodbye.

She left when my back was turned so I wouldn't have to watch her leave.

She spared my pain.

And she protected herself from it too.

It was the best thing for both of us—but it still hurt like hell.

———

I SAT on the couch in the living room with a bottle of aged scotch in front of me. It was a gift I'd received when we bought out a smaller chain of hotels so we could use their property to build our resorts. It was aged a hundred years—and so fucking smooth.

The elevator doors opened, and Coen walked inside. "Damn...I can tell you had a bad day."

"Something like that. What happened with you?"

"The judge ruled the prenup is valid."

I tried to grin, but I just couldn't. It wasn't possible. There was too much booze and depression in my veins. "Good. That bitch got what was coming to her."

Coen took the bottle out of my hands as he looked down at me in pity. "That's enough for the night, man. I'm guessing that means Monroe left?"

"Yep...left without saying goodbye."

"Only because it was too hard for her."

I glared at my brother. "When I walked through the door, she was disappointed I wasn't you."

"Only because I understand exactly what she's going through."

"It's not the same at all. I'm not Simone."

"But we both loved someone who didn't love us back," he snapped. "And that shit hurts."

"She loves me? She said that to you?"

"Not in those words. But, come on. You know it's true." He took a drink straight out of the bottle before he tightened the cap on the top. "You gave her a townhouse, and she threw a fit. Would a woman do that if she didn't love you? Anyone else would have taken the key with a ridiculous grin."

Even when she left, she still didn't want the place. She still wanted to stay here—with me.

"So, what now? Back to cherry popping?" He sat in the other armchair.

"No...those days are over."

"Good. Because if Simone figured it out, someone else might."

"That's not why I'm retiring."

"Then why?" He rested the bottle on his thigh, his fingers wrapped around the neck.

"It just doesn't feel right anymore."

"Then, what's your plan? Are you going to start dating? Because there's a perfectly perfect woman who already wants you." He indicated to the elevator, the last place she stood before she left my life forever.

"Not dating. Just fucking."

He sighed before he popped the lid and took a drink. "Simone broke my heart, and the last thing I want to do is fuck someone. She's a dumb bitch and I don't owe her anything, but I'm just not in that headspace. I'm telling you, when you screw someone, Monroe is going to be in your head the entire time."

Probably.

"You really want to be sitting here drinking your sorrows away?" he asked incredulously. "Or you could fix your sorrows right now."

"Just drop it, alright?" I didn't want to be told I was making a mistake. I knew what I was capable of, and I would never be capable of giving that woman what she deserved. "So, did you sign the divorce papers? Is it official?"

"No. She stormed out after the judge made his ruling."

"Drama queen."

"I haven't heard from her since. But I did get my place back."

"She got out?"

He nodded. "She must have gotten her own place because she gave me her key."

"Good. But I would have enjoyed you calling the cops on her."

"Yeah, I would have too. But I was thinking of staying here a little longer…"

"Why?" I asked, seeing no reason for him to share a penthouse with his brother.

He shrugged. "We're both in a dark place right now. Maybe we should be together, not apart."

"I'm not a pussy, and neither are you."

"Just an idea. But if you really want me to leave, I will."

My brother was about to get divorced, and I'd just lost a woman I already missed. Being together reminded me of the old times, when he would come over all the time and watch the game. We used to pick up women together, double date, and even share women. Having him around wouldn't be the worst thing in the world. "No…you should stay."

12

Monroe

I WAS IN WORSE SHAPE THAN THE LAST TIME HE LEFT.

And that was saying something because I was much better off this time around.

My debt was gone, I had a good job, and now I didn't have to pay rent at all. I owned a piece of property that had to be worth over five million dollars. It was big, beautiful, and it was so close to work, even a storm wouldn't make me take a cab.

I had it all.

But I felt like I had nothing at all.

The electricity had been turned on, so I had lights, running water, and heat. Winter was approaching, along with the freezing temperatures and chilly nights. All I had was an air mattress on the floor in front of the fireplace, but it still felt like a palace. With hardwood floors, high ceilings, and more space than I could possibly need, it was definitely a dream home. It could easily fit a family of four.

A family I would have with some other man.

I sat on the folding chair and drank the bottle of wine I'd bought for myself. I didn't have internet and I didn't want to use the data on my phone, so I only had my thoughts for entertainment. Unfortunately, all I could think about was the man who didn't want me, who preferred to go back to his old ways and forget about me.

How could he do all of this for me but not want me?

I would much rather keep all my debt and lose this house to have him instead.

He was all I needed to be happy.

The doorbell rang as I sat there with my gloomy thoughts.

It could only be one person since Slate was the only one who knew where I lived.

I left the bottle on the ground and headed to the front door. It was a large door, nine feet high, and it had a window on either side of the frame. I opened the door without bothering to check who was on the other side. It had to be him, and I didn't want to wait another second before I saw him.

Instead, it was Coen. I could feel my excitement melt away like a stick of butter in the microwave.

"Are you okay?" he asked, bundled up in his thick jacket.

"Yeah…I just thought you might be Slate."

"No. He's at home, drunk out of his mind."

"At least he's not out with someone else already…"

"He's not in that frame of mind at all." He looked over my shoulder and into the empty house. "So, can I come inside? I want to see the new place."

"Of course. I'm sorry." I stepped aside so he could get out of the freezing air.

"Wow, it's nice." He looked at the large staircase in the entryway and admired the chandelier hanging from the vaulted ceiling. Old wallpaper was on the walls, giving it a distinctly antique look. The place was at least fifty years old, but the appliances and bathrooms had been renovated.

"It's beautiful." I gave him a quick tour, showing him the living room, kitchen, and the bedrooms. "It's perfect."

"It is perfect. Big for one person, but I'm sure that will change in time."

I grabbed an extra chair so he could sit with me in the living room. "Eventually..." I pushed my air mattress aside so he wouldn't have to see my rumpled sheets and old tear stains. "Would you like some wine? I don't have any glasses, so I've been drinking it out of the bottle."

"I have low standards." He took the bottle from me and took a drink, not caring about my lipstick mark. "So, how are you?"

I gave him a ghostly expression, like I didn't care about anything at all anymore. I was an empty vase with no water or flowers. I was an empty chest that lacked a soul. I'd never wanted to be one of those people who lost the will to live when they experienced a breakup, but that was exactly how I felt. I felt stupid for thinking Slate would ever change. He said he would try to be something more—but not once did he try. I was the stupidest woman on the planet for believing him. "I've been better. You?"

He shrugged. "I've been better."

"How's the divorce going?"

"Judge ruled in my favor. She gets nothing."

"Good. I would have been surprised if he'd ruled in any other way."

"Now we just have to sign all the papers and actually get the divorce...but she stormed out. Haven't heard from her since."

"She's probably trying to figure out a way to get what she wants."

"Well, there is no way." He took a drink. "Unless she kills me." He chuckled like it was
absurd.

"Don't even say things like that..." Simone didn't seem like a murderer, but she'd already gone to intense extremes to get what she wanted. Who knew what she was capable of?

"I know she's a bitch, but she's not a murdering bitch."

I hoped so. "How is he?"

"He's a mess."

"He is?" I asked, trying not to sound too happy.

He nodded. "I don't get it. He's completely miserable, but he won't change his mind. He even got a little furious when he walked into your bedroom and you were hoping to see me instead of him. He looked like he wanted to rip my head off."

"Well…he's sensitive to that specific topic."

"I get that," he said. "But if you're that jealous over a woman, why let her go? Why spend millions on her? Why can't he pull his head out of his ass?"

"I told him I would only come back if he tried. He told me he would. But he never did…now I think he bought me these things because he feels guilty. He led me on and selfishly broke my heart."

Coen didn't have a rebuttal to that.

"I feel so stupid. I shouldn't have given him another chance."

"You had your debt wiped out because of it. Not to mention this place." He looked around the room.

"I would rather have an unbroken heart." I extended my hand to take the bottle back.

He leaned forward and handed it to me. "Not all hope is lost. Maybe he'll change his mind."

"The only reason he changed his mind last time was because he saw me with another guy. A handsome, wealthy guy. It pissed him off so much that he showed up at my work."

"And you don't mean anything to him…" He shook his head and chuckled. "No one's buying it, Slate."

"I am…" He wouldn't treat me like this if he really cared about me. I felt like a prostitute he picked up whenever he felt like it. I shouldn't have allowed him to do this to me. I should have been firmer about what I wanted. "So, you came here to check on me?"

"Yeah."

"Did he ask you to?"

"No. He doesn't know I'm here."

"Did you move out?"

"No. Simone gave up my penthouse, but I thought I would stay a little longer. He's been drinking a lot, and I'm worried about him. Not to mention, I'm depressed too. The idea of being alone in the penthouse I used to share with her...doesn't sound appealing. At least not right now."

"I know what you mean."

"I wonder if he would be jealous if he knew I were here...that asshole."

Slate was definitely the jealous type. "Probably."

Coen took the bottle back and took a few drinks. He fell quiet as he became lost in his thoughts.

I did the same thing, thinking about the crummy air mattress I would have to sleep on tonight. The worst part of it was—it wasn't Slate. I preferred sleeping on his hard chest over that air-inflated mattress. It was cold, uncomfortable, and lonely.

"You know...I have an idea. It's a bad idea. Terrible, actually. But...I can almost guarantee it will work."

"A terrible idea that will work?" I asked. "That sounds interesting."

"Nothing would make Slate angrier than seeing the two of us together. And not just because of what happened with Simone."

I couldn't believe what he was suggesting. "You're just starting to get along with your brother again. You really want to piss him off?"

"Yes, actually. I do want to piss him off. Because pissing him off will make him take action. If he thinks there's a chance something is going on between us, it'll drive him so crazy that he won't be able to see straight. He'll come running back."

"He came running back last time he was jealous, but it didn't get me anywhere."

"This time, it'll be different. This time, you'll tell him you want it all or nothing at all."

"I don't know…"

"I'm telling you, it'll work so well."

"You're really willing to risk your relationship with him?" I was prepared to do anything to get Slate to think logically, but not to ruin his newly restored relationship with his brother.

"When I tell him the truth later, he'll understand."

"It's still risky. You're just going to hope he catches us together? That'll infuriate him, especially after what happened with Simone. It'll just be tactless."

"No. This time, I'll talk to him about it. He always said he never cared that I wanted to be with Simone. If I'd just asked, he would have bowed out. He said it pissed him off that I snuck around behind his back. So if I I'm upfront about it, he can't get upset."

"But he will get upset."

"Good. Maybe that'll be enough to get him fired up."

"At you—not me."

"Not when I tell him we have a connection. We've been spending time together, and there's chemistry. He'll be extremely threatened. And if he gets angry, I'll tell him he should be with you. If it really bothers him that much, then it doesn't make sense for you not to be together."

It made perfect sense, but it could also blow up in our faces. "I really have no idea what his reaction will be. He'll definitely be pissed, but I don't know if that will get him to do anything."

"Since it's me, I think it will. I really do." He handed the bottle back to me. "So, you want to give it a try?"

I kept my mouth shut, unsure if I could go through with it.

"All I know is, that asshole is gonna sit around and drink and do nothing. Unless we do something, nothing will get done. Maybe he'll realize what he wants eventually, but by then, it might be too late. So, it's your call."

I wanted to at least try to make this work. If it didn't go anywhere and just pissed Slate off, we could tell him it was all a ploy to get us back together. Then I could move on... knowing we would never get back together. "Yeah...let's do it."

13

Slate

THE WEEK PASSED IN SLOW MOTION.

I did my daily routine, going to work, hitting the gym, and then sitting on the couch all night. I enjoyed my scotch and skipped dinner most of the time. Sometimes I was hungry, but I was not motivated to cook, so I snacked on whatever I could find. Even if it was filled with carbs, I didn't care.

I didn't care about anything anymore.

I'd never felt like this, like a piece of me was missing. I used to be the strong and unbreakable man who didn't need anyone, but now, I was lost and broken. That woman was just a transaction, but without her smell on my sheets and her smile on her lips, my life didn't have meaning.

I was a billionaire—but I'd never felt so poor.

Coen stayed with me, nursing his own depression over Simone. He didn't mention Monroe again. Didn't try to convince me to go after her. He seemed to have given up on me.

I was relieved but also disappointed.

I sat on one couch while he sat on the other. He scrolled through his phone while the game played on the TV. Our empty beer bottles were stacked on the coffee table, and the empty pizza box only had crumbs left over.

It'd been at least two years since I'd had pizza.

Coen lowered his phone and looked at me, ignoring the touchdown that had just happened on the screen. "You doing okay, man?"

"I'm fine." That was my automatic response to everything. I clearly wasn't fine, but I would stick to the bogus line to the end of my days. Even my assistant had asked me that question when I was at work yesterday, and that overstepped her boundaries.

"So, you still aren't going to work this out?"

"I thought we were done talking about that?"

He shrugged. "I just wanted to make sure you were sticking to your guns."

"Yes, I'm sticking to my guns."

He finished his beer before he set it on the table. "So, you're a hundred percent sure about that?"

It was an odd question, so I looked at him with my eyebrow raised. "What are you getting at, Coen?"

"Well...this is a little awkward. Not sure where to start." He rubbed his palms together as he ignored the TV and stared at the ground.

My mind jumped to conclusions, and my anger followed quickly behind. Coen took Simone behind my back, and now he wanted Monroe. They'd spent time together ever since he moved in here, and now I wondered what happened on the second story before Monroe relocated. After everything Coen and I had been through, would he stab me in the back again?

"I kinda have a thing for Monroe." He lifted his chin and met my gaze, anticipating my rage.

I stared at him blankly, unable to process the bullshit I was listening to. My nostrils flared like a pissed-off bull, and I wondered if I could throw him through the floor-to-ceiling windows and to the street hundreds of feet below.

"Nothing has happened, Slate." He held up his hand. "I would never go behind your back like that...not again."

I was too angry to speak. Insults ran rampant through my mind, but I couldn't voice a single one of them. Both of my hands formed fists, my knuckles turning white.

"I would never do anything unless you were okay with it. But if you guys are never going to work it out and you don't want her...I thought I would ask."

Still, my mouth wouldn't respond.

"She's always been so nice to me, even after what happened with Simone. She's easy to talk to, she's had her heart broken, she's pretty...I think she's really cool. You told me you wouldn't have cared about Simone if I'd told you I wanted to be with her. So that's why I'm telling you now."

My mouth finally unclenched so I could speak. "This isn't fucking Simone, Coen. Monroe isn't some gold-digging tramp. Monroe is a woman with class. She's a queen without a tiara. She's world-fucking-class. You don't deserve a woman like that."

"Maybe I don't. But you don't either. You say all these nice things about her, but you still don't want to be with her? It's just empty words, Slate. If she's really that amazing, you wouldn't have let her go."

"Fuck you, asshole."

He didn't flinch at my venom. "Is that a yes or a no?"

"What do you think?" I snapped. "We just broke up a week ago."

"Because you dumped her." He met my fire with his own. "You didn't want her anymore. It's not like she broke up with you. If you don't want her, then why can't I ask her out? You can't say you have feelings for her if you don't want to be with her. That's just not right."

"Why are you so obsessed with my leftovers?"

The corner of his mouth rose in a smile. "Simone manipulated me. But Monroe is the perfect woman. I've been with a lying tramp, so I know Monroe is nothing like that. I appreciate her goodness, her kindness. I'm looking for a good woman to settle down with, and that's exactly what she is."

"Go fuck yourself, Coen. After everything I've done for you, you pull this stunt?"

"I'm not pulling anything." He leaned forward. "I'm asking you. If you say no, then I'll back off. But if you say yes…I'm going for it. So, what's it going to be?"

My eyes shifted back and forth as I looked into his, livid at my brother's second betrayal. He didn't go behind my back and try to fuck her like he did with Simone, but it still made me angry. If I said no, he would abandon this and forget about it. But that wasn't enough for me. "You're a piece of shit, you know that?"

"I'll take that as a no."

"You're an asshole for even asking."

"Am I?" he countered. "You're the asshole who broke that woman's heart. She said you were going to try to be something more, and you didn't even make an attempt. It was just empty words so you could keep using her. Maybe I'm an asshole for wanting my brother's ex, but at least I don't play games like you."

"I did try," I snapped. "It's just not for me."

"Then why can't I date her?" he snapped. "You don't want her, never wanted to really be with her, so why can't I ask her out? I actually like her. I want to take her out to dinner and get to know her. I don't just want to fuck her. I want a wife—a real wife this time. I'm a successful, honest, and wealthy guy. If you want her to end up with someone good, who's better than me?"

I shook my head, disgusted by his reasoning. "No."

His eyes filled with disappointment. "You're an even bigger asshole than I thought."

"I'm the asshole?" I asked incredulously. "You want to fuck my ex-girlfriend a week after we broke up."

"No. A week after you *dumped* her. And she was never your girlfriend. You paid her for sex—end of story. You can't have it both ways. You can't say she meant nothing to you and she was just living here because she needed a place to stay, but then switch to a whole different story when you don't want me to have her. That's a dick move."

"You want to talk about dick moves, huh?" I had more ammunition than he could take. He'd fucked me over royally, more than anyone else I'd ever known. Just the fact that he had the audacity to initiate this conversation was ridiculous.

"Look, I think she likes me too. She and I have been talking a lot, and we have a lot in common. She's heartbroken over you, and I'm heartbroken over Simone. We both got played by people we loved—"

"I never played her."

"It seems that way—to both of us."

"And she doesn't like you." I remembered walking into her bedroom and the way she hoped I was my brother. It hurt me deeply, made me so jealous that I didn't know how to respond. Simone and Coen hurt me so much with their betrayal, and now I felt like I was living through it again.

"Maybe she doesn't like me the way she likes you. But I can see it going somewhere. I was at her place a few days ago—"

"What?" My brother was already sneaking off to her place while I sat on the couch and moped?

"I stopped by to check it out. It's nice. We sat in the living room on plastic chairs, shared a bottle of wine, and just talked. I'm telling you, we have a lot in common."

"You can have anything in common if you try hard enough."

"Maybe," he said. "But it doesn't change the way I feel. I see it going somewhere. I don't see us doing anything serious right this second, but I can see feelings developing. I can see chemistry. So I thought I would ask now before all of that stuff does develop. Maybe I'm jumping the gun right now, but I would rather be as honest as possible instead of betraying you again."

I wanted to break my beer bottle and stab him with it. "How thoughtful…"

"Slate, if it bothers you that much, you can still get her back. She's yours for the taking if you want her."

I turned back to the TV, knowing that wasn't an option. I'd been in a relationship once, and it had ended so badly. Now the past seemed to be repeating itself—and it was nearly identical. My trust issues only deepened. A part of me knew Monroe was different, that she was honest and loyal and would never hurt me. This was only happening because I was the one who hurt her. It was easier to sabotage the relationship before she had the chance to hurt me.

"Slate."

I turned back to him.

"If she's your woman, make her your woman. But if not…then I think you're being the asshole by not letting her be happy."

"You're pretty arrogant to assume you would make her happy."

"I've been her shoulder to cry on, and she's been mine."

I hated the idea of her running to him for comfort, but I couldn't expect her to run to me instead. Instead of letting her hurt me, I hurt her. It was the only way I could protect myself.

"What's your answer, man?"

"You know my answer."

"Well, that's pretty fucked up if you ask me. But fine." Coen rose to his feet and walked out of the living room, abandoning me and all the garbage on the table. He headed upstairs and left me alone on the couch.

To suffer my rage in silence.

COEN and I didn't speak for days.

I was too pissed off to even look at him, and he was smart enough to steer clear of me.

I was so livid, I actually wanted to punch him.

Hadn't decided if I would or not.

I was sitting in my office when he stepped inside, probably choosing to speak to me in public instead of behind closed doors where I could punch his face in. To the best of my knowledge, Coen hadn't tried to contact Monroe since I told him he couldn't ask her out.

If he did it anyway, I might kill him.

He stepped inside and dropped a folder on my desk. "Simone is missing."

My hostility disappeared for a moment. "Missing?"

"I've been wanting to sign our divorce papers and move on, but she's nowhere to be found. I've asked her parents, and they say they haven't seen her either."

"I wonder what that's about?"

He shrugged. "No idea. I can file for divorce without her, but it would take longer. It's easier just to get her signatures on a few pages and be done with it."

"Maybe she's ashamed." As she should be.

"Simone has never been ashamed of anything before."

"Good point."

"Maybe she's going to try to convince you to give it another try…since she's left with nothing."

"Five million dollars isn't nothing," he said with a chuckle.

"But her legal defense must have been a few hundred grand."

He slid his hands into his pockets. "She'll turn up soon. I just hope nothing happened to her."

I raised an eyebrow.

"I hate the bitch, but I don't want her to be dead."

"Because the police would assume you were the one who did it?"

"No...but that's a good point." He lingered in front of my desk like he had more to say but didn't know how to spit it out. He probably wanted to talk about Monroe since that was the reason for our newfound tension. He must have thought the better of it because he didn't mention it. "That's all the paperwork I got from the construction guys in Jackson Hole. All the foundation has been laid. They're ready to build."

"Great."

He nodded before he walked out.

I was pissed at my brother for even thinking Monroe was an option, but I was also relieved he'd asked me before going for it. And I was relieved he'd listened to my answer. Because the idea of the two of them together made me sick to my stomach. The idea of Monroe being with anyone made me sick to my stomach...

———

AFTER I HIT the gym and showered, I kept thinking about Monroe.

It'd been over a week since we last spoke.

I hoped she was doing okay in her new place. She was sleeping alone every night, just as I was. I hoped she wasn't afraid. I hoped she didn't fear someone would break in again. She lived in a nice neighborhood with constant police surveillance, so she should have nothing to worry about.

But I wanted to check on her anyway.

I missed her like crazy. I missed the sound of her voice, the softness of her smile. I missed the way she rose on her tiptoes to kiss me when I walked in the door. I missed burying my nose in hair and smelling her perfume.

I missed everything.

I grabbed my coat then left for her townhouse. I didn't ask

my driver to take me because it was such a short walk. It was just across the street and a few blocks over. Knowing she was so close to me comforted me, because I could get to her quickly if she ever needed me.

Ten minutes later, I arrived at her doorstep.

I rang the doorbell and stood in the cold air with my jacket wrapped tightly around me. There were fewer people on the street than usual because people forked over cash to take a cab when it got this cold.

I chose to walk because I needed some time to prepare for this moment. I shouldn't be here. My visit was completely self-ish. Seeing me would only make it harder for her, but not seeing her was making it harder for me.

Her footsteps sounded a moment later. When they stopped, I knew she was looking through the peephole right at me. She probably lost her breath at my unexpected appearance, thinking she would never see me again.

A moment later, she opened the door.

Pain sprinkled her eyes like stars in the sky. She wasn't overtly surprised, but she didn't give me any warmth either, as if this visit were completely unexpected. She kept her hand on the door like she needed something to hold on to. She was dressed in a thin red sweater that fit her hourglass frame wonderfully. The V-neck at the front hinted at her beautiful flesh and sexy tits. Her black jeans were snug and tight, molding to her sculpted legs perfectly. She was sexier than I remembered—and it'd only been a week since I'd last seen her.

Words failed me.

She found her footing first. "Hi…" That beautiful voice was soft like a rose petal.

Now I missed her even more. "Hi."

"Uh, you want to come in?" She opened the door wider, revealing the staircase and chandelier behind her.

"Yeah." I stepped inside and wiped my shoes on the rug.

"I thought I would check on you…see how you like your new place."

"Oh…" She didn't hide her disappointment, as if she were hoping I'd stopped by for a different reason.

That was exactly what I feared.

"Well, I love it. I don't have any furniture, but it's still cozy."

"Diane told me it'll be here in a few weeks. She expedited everything."

"As long as I have my air mattress and some wine, I'm fine." She crossed her arms over her chest, purposely guarded now that she knew I was there for platonic reasons. That spark in her eyes had been extinguished. Nothing but pitch black remained behind.

Now I felt like a dick for stopping by. I was only there because I missed looking at her face, missed seeing those beautifully painted lips. I didn't intend to screw her on that air mattress, but now that I was face-to-face with her, I wouldn't mind a kiss.

But that would be cruel.

Footsteps sounded from the other room.

My eyes flicked into the living room in front of the fire-place, and then my brother came into view. With a glass of wine in his hand and dressed in jeans and a long-sleeved shirt, he looked comfortable in her living room, like they'd been drinking for hours.

The need for affection died away—replaced by blood lust.

Coen was in her townhouse—after I told him he couldn't have her.

He'd directly disobeyed me.

I felt my body stiffen everywhere, felt my eyes focus on him like two lasers. My muscles pumped with the increase in blood flow. Adrenaline prepared me for the fight about to take place. My knuckles ached to leave imprints in his cheekbones.

Monroe disrupted my frenzy with her sweet voice. "I

invited Coen for some wine. He told me Simone has disappeared off the map…which is concerning."

My eyes turned back to hers, unable to believe what I'd just heard.

She invited him?

Was Coen right? That they really did get along that well? I couldn't believe that she wanted to screw my brother, but I could believe she was using him to feel better. But once the pain started to fade away, she would see him in a new light.

And then the past would repeat itself.

I stared at her without speaking, feeling the pain carve me like a knife. If I let her go, she would end up with someone else. But not just anyone else—my brother. The holidays would be spent with this woman at the table, her hand held in Coen's. They would get married, and then she would be pregnant with his child.

She would let him fuck her.

My brother would fuck my woman.

My eyes turned back to Coen.

He behaved like he'd done nothing wrong, and if her story was true, then he really did do nothing wrong. She invited him over, and that was why he believed he had a chance with her. There was a glimmer of hope there.

Logic faded away, and all I felt was rage. Cold, merciless rage. I knocked the glass out of his hand, and it shattered on the floor with an audible crash. Before he could anticipate my moves, my fist was in buried in his face with enough force to break his skull in two. I gripped the front of his shirt and slugged him two more times before either of them could figure out what was happening.

"Slate!" Monroe grabbed me by the arm and yanked me back. "Stop!"

She was too weak to do anything, so I gripped him by the throat and punched him again, this time making his nose bleed.

"Slate!" She jumped on my back and locked her arms around my throat. "Stop it! Now!"

Coen twisted out of my grasp and fell back, his eyes already swollen and blood dripping down his face. "She invited me, asshole. Calm the fuck down."

"She's mine. I told you she was mine, so back off." I felt Monroe crawl down my back now that the fight was over.

"Yours?" Coen asked incredulously. "She's not yours, asshole. She's not mine either. I can come over here whenever the hell I want as her friend. You need a reality check, Slate. Big time." He wiped his nose on the back of his forearm and walked into the kitchen, probably to clean himself up.

I breathed so hard my chest started to ache from the contractions. My nostrils were flared to twice their size, and I was still so livid I couldn't think straight. I could feel my pulse everywhere, from my ears to the veins in my back.

"Slate." Monroe's voice came from behind me, heavy with pain.

I slowly turned around and faced her, and I felt ashamed the second I looked at the disappointment in her eyes.

"I think it's best if we don't see each other anymore..." Her eyes watered noticeably as she spoke, just as they did when I'd ended our relationship. "You can't come by here anymore. You can't care if I'm friends with your brother. You can't throw a hissy fit every time you get jealous...not when I don't mean anything to you. You're playing with me...and I don't like it."

"I'm not playing with you—"

"You did the exact same thing with Wyatt. You didn't want me, but when someone else did, you got jealous. You don't want me, but you don't want anyone else to have me either. You want to keep me on your leash, keep me heartbroken as long as possible."

"That's not true—"

"Get out. I don't want to see you ever again."

Breaking up with her was hard enough, but hearing her cut me out of her life for good was worse. "Monroe——"

"I'm not Simone. I'll never be Simone. I'm a good and loyal person. If you don't already know that about me, then you're a lost cause. I'm going to start dating again. I'm going to start sleeping with other guys. I'm not going to stop looking for the man I want to sleep with every night for the rest of my life. If that's not you, then that means he's out there somewhere. I'm going to find him. Don't you dare get in my way."

14

Monroe

"THAT PLAN DID NOT WORK." I SAT IN THE PLASTIC CHAIR and drank straight from the bottle.

Coen had his own bottle, and he sat across from me while the fire burned in the fireplace. "I think it did work."

"He almost broke your nose."

He had a tampon stuffed in one nostril. "It was worth it. It forced him to confront his real feelings. He wasn't livid that I betrayed him. He was heartbroken that you might have already moved on. That had nothing to do with me."

"I think it had a little to do with you."

"But not much." He drank from the bottle. "And that little speech you gave really sank deep inside him."

"I meant every word."

"As you should. A real woman doesn't wait around for a guy. And if you ask me, Slate isn't worth waiting around for. I know he can be the man you want...but he needs a push."

"A big push."

"I'm telling you, that plan either worked or it didn't. There's no in-between."

It was safe to say it didn't work. I told Slate I never wanted to see him again, and he didn't argue with me. I told him I wanted to find someone else to spend my life with, and that didn't get him to change his mind. He was so stubborn that he couldn't even see his own feelings. "I hate him…"

"No, you don't."

"Then I hate myself. I hate myself for falling for someone who will never feel the same way."

"He does feel the same way."

"If he won't admit it out loud, then it doesn't count. If he never acts on those feelings, he's just a coward."

"You got that part right. He is a coward."

"I can't believe how much Simone screwed him up…" That woman was so foul, I didn't understand how Slate trusted her in the first place. He was much younger than he was now, and she was the first person he'd ever slept with, but he seemed too smart to let an evil woman affect him.

"Yeah. I was with her for five years, married to her, used by her, and I don't think I would have a problem trusting someone else. What are the odds that what happened with Simone would ever happen again? He's such a strong guy, I'm surprised it bothers him so much."

"I know he doesn't want to look like a fool again…but acting this way is making him look like a huge fool."

He raised his bottle. "I'll drink to that."

"But I guess I have to give up on him…"

He drank from the bottle and stared at the fire.

"I don't want to, but I can't keep waiting for him to get his shit together."

"I agree. You're amazing and deserve to be with a guy who appreciates you. Unfortunately, my brother doesn't fit the bill. I was hoping you guys would work out since you make him so happy…but I guess that's not going to happen."

That meant I would have to go out, meet new people, and start over. But I suspected I wouldn't find a man I connected with so well. With Slate, I felt so safe, like nothing could ever hurt me.

Well, except Slate himself.

"I need to move on too. I'm not too excited about it, but I've got to put myself out there."

"I figured you would be excited to get laid."

He shook his head. "I used to be all about that before Simone, but after I was in a monogamous relationship, I realized how much I liked it. I like being with one person. People say the sex grows stale, but I disagree. You learn what the other person likes, and you grow."

I smiled. "That's kinda sweet."

He shrugged. "I guess I'm a romantic guy. Well, I was... until my wife stabbed me in the back. But I'm sure there's a better woman out there. At least I didn't waste another five years before I realized what Simone really was. I'm not going to let her ruin my life the way she ruined Slate's."

"Good. Too bad Slate doesn't see it that way."

"You want to head to the bars with me tomorrow?" he asked. "I can be your wingman, and you can be mine."

"The bar scene...I've never done that before." I didn't get out much before I met Slate. I was a virgin for so long for a reason.

"Just put on a black cocktail dress and look pretty. They'll come to you."

"And what do I say?"

"Talk to them if you think they're cute. Blow them off if you don't. Pretty simple."

"I don't know...seems like it's too soon." I gripped the bottle in my hands and remembered the nights when it was just the two of us, moving together under the sheets. That's what I wanted more than anything, to be back with the man I adored.

"You told him you weren't going to wait around," he reminded me. "You told him you were going to look for the right guy. You gave him everything, and he was the one who teased you."

"Yes…"

"So, go out. Meet someone. Maybe you'll meet someone you really like. Maybe you won't. Doesn't hurt to try."

"Yeah…maybe." I sat at the bar the first time we broke up, and Wyatt appeared out of thin air. We struck up a conversation and hit it off pretty quickly. I could call him again, but that seemed strange contacting him when Slate dumped me the second time. Made me seem a little desperate. "So, he was pissed when you told him you wanted to ask me out?"

"Livid."

"But that wasn't enough?"

He shrugged. "I guess not. Maybe if he thinks you're seeing someone else and he can't stop it, that'll get his ass in gear."

I didn't want to play games. I didn't want him to come back to me only because he was jealous. I wanted him to come back to me because he realized he didn't want to live without me for another day. I wanted to be the woman he wanted for the rest of his life. I wanted to be something more to him than just a transaction.

I wanted to be his everything.

But if that hadn't happened by now, it was never going to happen.

15

Slate

I FELT SO MANY THINGS AT ONCE.

Rage. Blood lust. Murder.

But I also felt pain, sadness, and despair.

I felt everything at every single moment of the day. It didn't matter if I were at home or at the office. It didn't matter if I were in the shower or in bed. The regret was constant. She ordered me out of her life like she couldn't stand me any longer, like I was the sole cause of all her pain.

I was the reason for her tears.

On top of that, I was pissed at my brother. Even if nothing was going on between them, I didn't like knowing they were together behind closed doors. I didn't like their deep conversations into the night. I told Coen I would never give my blessing for him to be with Monroe, and I hoped he would take that request seriously.

I'd die if I had to see them together.

Coen and I didn't talk for days, and when we did see each other, we ignored the bruises all over his face. It took a few days for his right eye to stop looking so black. His nose healed quicker and went back to normal, but it was still obvious he was in a fight. But we didn't actually speak to each other.

I was pissed at him. He was pissed at me.

Surprisingly enough, he still stayed at the penthouse with me. He could return to his place whenever he wanted, but he stuck around. Maybe he was trying to prove to me he wasn't having Monroe over in the middle of the night or going to her place.

That didn't sound like something Monroe would do, so I wasn't worried about it.

On Thursday night, he came downstairs dressed like he was ready to go out. He was in a gray V-neck with a black blazer on top. He wore his fitted jeans and black boots. His Omega watch was on his wrist and his wedding ring forgotten.

I stared at him without speaking, still refusing to talk to him.

"I'm going out tonight. Thought it was time to get back on the horse."

"Is Monroe the horse?" I hissed.

He brushed off the insult. "No. I'm not sure who the horse is yet."

"Just hope it's not an actual horse."

The corner of his mouth rose in a smile. "There's still no sign of Simone and I'm not legally divorced yet, but I thought it was time to move on with my life. So Monroe and I are going out to try our luck at a bar."

My neck cracked because I turned my head in his direction so quickly. "What?"

"I'm Monroe's wingman, and she's my wing woman."

Now I was pissed off all over again, and Coen wasn't even trying to fuck her. "Are you serious?"

"Yes. We both agreed it was time to get on with our lives."

"So, let me get this straight." I rose to my feet. "You're taking my woman out so a bunch of jackasses can hit on her?"

"She's not your woman, man. Get over it."

My eyes narrowed. "It's still fucked up. You're taking my ex out so she can meet a bunch of guys while I'm miserable over here? Shouldn't you be taking me out?"

"Do you want to go out?" he asked, his eyebrow raised.

Actually, no. The last thing I wanted to do was go out and fuck pussy. I hadn't gotten hard once over these past few weeks. Why would I want to fuck someone when I could barely sleep? "No."

"Then why can't I go out with her? She's my friend."

"I'm your brother. You really don't see how this is a violation of decency?"

"So I can't have any contact with her?" he asked incredulously. "I asked your permission to ask her out, which you failed to give. I respected your wishes. Now, I'm only her friend and nothing more. But yet, I'm still doing something wrong."

"I don't want her going out to bars and picking up guys. There's nothing but assholes out there."

"Well, you dumped her, so it's really none of your business." He straightened his watch and stepped back. "We're going to the Oak Room if you want to join us. If not, have a good night." He headed to the elevator and hit the button.

I couldn't believe this was happening. Imagining Monroe getting hit on by every guy in New York made me want to rip out my own throat. She would look beautiful in a black dress with heels, and she could have any guy she wanted. Last time she went to a bar, she picked up one of the richest and most eligible bachelors in the country.

Who would she pick up this time?

16

Monroe

My heart was beating a million miles a minute. I wore a backless black dress, something Slate bought for me, so I felt awkward wearing it to meet someone new. But I had nothing else to wear for the time being.

Coen looked handsome in his blazer and V-neck, and right off the bat, all the women in the bar were looking at him. I couldn't blame them, not when he looked so similar to his older brother. They had the same beautiful masculinity, with broad shoulders and powerful jawlines. Their bodies were flanked with muscles, and their eyes steamed like hot coffee in the morning. It was ironic that they looked so similar but I wasn't attracted to Coen at all. "What did Slate say when you told him we were doing this?"

Coen shrugged. "He was upset, but not enough to actually stop it."

This was my last attempt to make him chase me, and it failed. It was officially over. If none of this made Slate come to his senses, then nothing would. Tonight was the first night of the rest of my life.

"Don't think about him." Coen held his Old Fashioned in his hand. "You're the sexiest chick in this bar, and you can have any guy you want. If Slate doesn't want you, that's his loss. Forget about him."

"You take my side a lot even though he's your brother."

"I love him, and I'll have his back forever. But he's a complete douchebag. You deserve better."

"Well...thanks." I clinked my glass against his.

He took a long drink before he set the glass on the table. "There are a ton of guys looking at you. I think the only reason they haven't come over is because of me. So, see anyone you like? I'll talk you up."

I turned around and looked. At one booth, there was a group of guys sitting together, all wearing suits like they just got off work. One was particularly handsome, with nice brown hair and blue eyes. He had a muscular build similar to Slate's. I told myself I shouldn't compare, but I knew exactly what I liked. "I like that guy in the middle..."

"Alright. I'll talk you up."

"See anyone you like?"

"That blonde over there is pretty hot."

I saw her standing near the bathroom, with sky-high heels and a red dress. "She's staring at you."

"So she should be easy prey. I'll talk to your guy and send him over before I make the kill." He stepped away from the bar.

"Whoa, hold on. What do I say to him?"

"Try hello. Introduce yourself." He walked away.

"Coen?"

He ignored me and approached their table.

I faced forward and tried to keep my cool. My drink was in front of me, so I kept sipping it, letting the booze warm my stomach and destroy my nerves. I was nervous because I was jumping into something new, but it also felt right because I couldn't wait for Slate to actually care about me. To him, I would always be a commodity, something that could be bought. I needed a man who saw me as a person, a woman, a soul mate. Maybe it was too soon for me to move on, but after the way he'd treated me, could anyone really blame me?

Coen returned a second later, the handsome man at his side. "Monroe, this is Hugh. Hugh, this is my friend Monroe. She's a fan of the Yankees, loves pizza, and works in fashion. You two have fun." He left us alone and approached the blonde he'd had his eyes on earlier.

Hugh leaned against the bar and eyed my drink. "Can I get you a refill?"

"Sure."

"I like a woman who enjoys a good drink. You have Old Fashioneds often?"

"Only when I'm nervous."

"Why are you nervous?" He had a nice smile and soothing presence about him. He was so calm it seemed like he did this frequently, talked to strangers in bars. He had classically handsome features, so he probably put the moves on gorgeous women all the time. He appeared to be out of my league.

"I haven't been out in a long time."

"Bad breakup, huh?"

"It wasn't really bad…it was just a breakup."

"So you're in the stage where you're forcing yourself to go out?"

"Pretty much."

"Been there, done that." He glanced at Coen in the corner. "Your friend said you thought I was cute."

"That's correct. I do think you're cute."

"Well, I think you're gorgeous, so we have something in common."

I did my best not to let my cheeks flush with heat. "Thanks…"

"So, are you looking for a one-night stand or just pleasant conversation?"

"That's blunt," I asked with a laugh.

"I just like to know what I'm dealing with."

"Do you get a lot of women asking for one-night stands?"

He shrugged. "I don't kiss and tell."

"Ooh…a gentleman."

He drank from his glass, his eyes staying focused on me. "So, what are you interested in?"

"Well, if you're going to be blunt, so am I. I'm looking for the man I'll spend the rest of my life with. I don't expect to meet him tonight or next week…but that's what I'm looking for. I'm not a one-night stand kind of girl. I've actually only been with one guy."

He nodded slowly. "There's nothing wrong with that."

"I know. What are you looking for?"

"Nothing in particular. Wherever the wind takes me. For the most part, I'm having fun right now. But if I met an amazing woman who rocked my world, I'd marry her tomorrow. My future is an open book."

"I like that." I hated hearing men swear off marriage just because they thought they wouldn't like it. This guy was open to anything, and he was honest about everything too. "Your story is unwritten."

"Exactly." He clinked his glass against mine. "I was—"

"Get the fuck away from her." His masculine voice was filled with imminent threat, like he had a gun stashed in his jacket, fully loaded. He came right up behind the man I was speaking with, several inches taller than him, and with black oil in his eyes. "Now."

Hugh stepped aside and looked over his shoulder. "Let me guess. The ex-boyfriend—"

"I'll shove that glass up your ass if you don't walk away right now." Slate stood his ground, his musculature undeniable even in his coat. The shadow on his jawline accentuated his features even more. He looked like a man possessed by the devil.

"Slate!" I smacked his ass. "Don't talk to him like that."

Slate ignored me and continued to stare down my admirer. "Now."

In a small act of defiance, Hugh looked at me. "It was nice to meet you. Take care." He kept his cool and walked back to the table where his friends were waiting.

Now I was even more furious with Slate. "I told you I never wanted to see you again—"

"This has tortured me every single day. Every morning when I wake up, I think it's going to get easier, and it never does." One arm rested on the bar while the other gripped the back of my chair. He boxed me in so I had nowhere to go. "Coen told me he wanted to date you, and that was a nightmare in itself. But knowing you're out here picking up guys... makes me sick to my stomach."

None of this made me feel better. It only made me feel worse. "You can't throw a fit every time you get jealous—"

"I'm not throwing a fit—not this time." He lowered his voice so only I could hear. "I'm miserable without you. I haven't even been tempted to go back to my old ways. I haven't wanted to go out and pick up someone new. All I do is stay home and drink until the pain stops...but it never does." His eyes shifted back and forth as they looked into mine. "You were right about me. I do have trust issues. That bitch fucked me up pretty bad. She made me look like a fool to the entire world and ripped my family apart. The worst part of it was losing my brother—not losing her. I haven't been able to get close to anyone ever since, not a single soul. I turned into a gargoyle, a statue that sits in his castle and watches everyone else live their lives. I paid for sex because it gave me all the control. But then I met you...and I wanted to keep you without losing that control."

I hung on every word, wanting to forgive him and go back to his place. But then I remembered that nothing had changed, that he'd pulled this stunt once before. "You did the same thing when I met Wyatt. You told me you were going to try, and you never did. Nothing was different, and you treated me like something you paid for."

"Cherry, I know——"

"It won't be any different this time. You've already hurt me twice now, and I won't survive a third time."

"I won't hurt you again."

I wanted to believe those big, brown eyes. "Yes, you will. Jealousy brought you here, not love. You don't want me, but you don't want anyone else to have me. I'm a piece of property, and you want people off your land. It's...disgusting."

His eyes narrowed in agony.

"I'm looking for love. I'm looking for a good man. I'm looking for trust, commitment, devotion. You're too damaged to offer me those things. You're too distrusting. I've been honest and loyal from the very beginning, but you've never trusted me. That will never change. You'll never change."

His jaw tightened as the pain filled his eyes.

"We want different things. You want domination, control, ownership...I want love. Goodbye, Slate." I grabbed my drink and slid off the chair. I headed to the table where the man had returned to his friends. I refused to look back at the disappointed look on Slate's face. I had to focus on the future, on moving on. He was only there because jealousy made him territorial. He wasn't there because he loved me, because he couldn't live without me.

He was just a selfish asshole.

17

Slate

I DIDN'T REALIZE HOW LATE IT WAS UNTIL JILLIAN CAME into my office. "We're leaving for the day. Is there anything else I can get you before we take off?"

I glanced at the clock and realized it was almost six. "No, enjoy your weekend."

"You too, Mr. Remington." She walked out with the other assistants.

I stayed at my desk because I had nowhere to go. My brother was still living with me, and I didn't want to face him. Now when I looked at him, I thought of Monroe. I hadn't asked how their night went. I didn't ask if Monroe went home with that pretty boy because I couldn't swallow the answer.

I'd never felt so terrible in my life.

I had the strangest sensation in my throat. It was constantly constricting, constantly getting tight and warm. My heart seemed to grow several times bigger, and my chest could barely contain it any longer. My body was out of whack because it was so focused on fighting the pain.

If only I could take a Vicodin for this.

I looked out the glass window to the city behind. Now that it was winter, it was already dark by five. The city was illuminated with glorious lights all over the place. I had nowhere to go and no purpose, so I sat there and watched the city thrive while I stopped living altogether.

I couldn't straighten out my thoughts or feelings. I went after Monroe, but she rejected me. She didn't want me, not after I'd pulled too many stunts. She had been the only woman in my life for the past three months, and because of her, the rest of my life would be different. Even if I could never have her again, I wouldn't go back to my previous way of living. I wouldn't go back to fucking virgins and paying for the experience. Now, when I thought about my past, I was disgusted with myself. I was such an asshole when we first met, from our introduction in this office to the dinner we had shortly afterward. I didn't treat her with respect. It only happened when she demanded it.

She changed me.

She made me into a better man, a different man.

And she did it in such a short amount of time.

I could never go back to what I used to be. But I couldn't picture myself meeting a nice woman and falling in love.

Not when I'd already met a nice woman.

A perfect woman.

A woman who loved me for me, despite my flaws and not because of my money.

Why the fuck did I throw her away?

Why didn't I trust her?

Why did I let that bitch ruin my past as well as my future?

I'd never been so disappointed in myself.

My back was to the door, so I didn't notice my brother until he walked inside. "Forget how to knock?"

"I saw Jillian in the lobby. She said you were still here… staring out the window."

"Yeah, I've been doing that a lot lately."

"Why haven't you gone home yet?"

I faced the window again. "What for? There's nothing there."

"I hope you don't feel that way because of me. Because I can leave."

I crossed my legs and rested my arms on the armrests. "I don't want to hear about your night last night."

"You mean, you don't want to hear about Monroe's night…"

I stared at my building across the street, seeing my penthouse on the top floor.

"I went to the blonde's place. Being with someone else was weird at first, but after the initial shock, it felt good. I'm glad I put myself out there…even though I'm still technically married. If Simone wouldn't be such a pussy, I could divorce her already."

Did Monroe go home with Pretty Boy? Did she take him back to her townhouse and screw him on the air mattress? Did they do it in front of the fireplace while the frost drew patterns on the windows?

It made me want to shoot myself.

"I know you don't want to know about Monroe, but I'll tell you anyway—"

"Don't. I'll put a bullet in my brain—"

"She went home alone. We shared a cab with her on the drive home."

I felt my lungs expand with the deep breath I took. The relief gave me a high.

"But she got the guy's number, and I think she's going to see him again."

The relief vanished instantly. That high disappeared like a candle had just been blown out. "I tried to work it out. I went there and poured out my heart to her."

"I remember you threatening the guy she was talking to and not really saying anything you hadn't already said before.

I don't blame her for not giving you another chance. She's not settling for less than what she deserves."

"And what's that?"

"The whole nine yards. Love, marriage, kids. If you aren't interested in that, then it'll never work anyway."

I'd never given much thought to having children, but I wasn't averse to the concept. Getting to trust someone enough to start a family was the problem. Simone and Coen had battered me hard. Even now, I couldn't let it go entirely.

"So, I think this is for the best. You want completely different things. She deserves to have everything she wants... even if you're the man she wants all of that with."

"She said that?" I stared at my penthouse, the windows dark because they were tinted.

"Yes."

"She said she wants to spend her life with me?"

"Is it not obvious to you, Slate? Is it not obvious that this woman is head over heels for you? Let me paint a picture for you, alright? You're Simone...and Monroe is me. You keep playing her like a fool, and she keeps coming back because she loves you. But now, she's finally realized you're just going to keep hurting her over and over."

Those words hit me right in the chest, dug deep like a hook had been inserted right under the skin. Simone humiliated me, and in the end, I did the same thing to Monroe. She was open and honest with me, and I kept using her for what I wanted. I told her I would try to be something more, and I never did. I lied to her, unknowingly. She was good to me, and I was never good to her.

It hit me hard then.

I couldn't make myself trust her...but she was the one who shouldn't trust me.

18

Monroe

I WALKED HOME FROM WORK WITH THE PHONE PRESSED TO my ear. "How'd it go with the blonde?"

"Good. She gives great head."

"Coen! A gentleman doesn't kiss and tell."

"Hey, you asked."

"I meant, did you have a good time?"

"I got a blow job. So yes, I had a great time."

I chuckled then crossed the street as I approached my townhouse. "You're gross."

"I'm a man. We're all gross. What about Hugh? He seems hunky and dreamy."

"Did you just say hunky and dreamy?"

"Uh…shit. I did. Let's just forget that happened."

I laughed as I pulled out my keys from my pocket. "Yes, I'll carry your secret because that was very embarrassing."

"So, you like the guy?"

"There wasn't anything I didn't like about him…" I got the door opened and walked inside.

"That doesn't sound good."

"No, he's great. Really. He's just not…"

"Slate?" he asked. "Yeah, I understand."

"Did he ask about the evening at all?"

"Not really."

I locked the door behind me and set my things on the kitchen counter. I still had no furniture, so the counter was cluttered with my things. I set my jacket on the counter and kept the phone against my ear.

"But he's pretty beat up about it. I've never seen him so low. He stays late at work and just stares out the window."

I hated hurting him, but I couldn't let him hurt me any longer. I had to get out of that dead-end relationship before I was stuck there forever, perpetually heartbroken. "He'll get over it."

"Maybe. Maybe not."

"Well...I guess that's that, then." It was really over. I was proud of myself for not giving in to Slate, but I was still miserable without him. The first serious relationship I'd had with a man turned out to be the biggest mistake. I loved someone who was incapable of loving me. I loved someone who was so emotionally unstable, they paid to fuck virgins. I should have seen the red flags a long time ago.

"I'm sorry."

"Me too." I felt the tears burning behind my eyelids, so I ended the conversation before he could hear the tears in my throat. I set the phone on the counter and closed my eyes as I fought against the involuntary emotion that took over. I gripped the edges, breathed a few times, and managed to stifle my tears, but not before a few drops broke through. My eyes watered and a few tears dripped down my cheek, but they didn't turn into heavy sobs. I wiped my face with my fingers then cleared my throat.

The doorbell rang.

I'd just gotten off the phone with Coen, so I knew it wasn't him.

That left one person.

Unless it was a Girl Scout selling cookies…that would be wonderful.

I was tempted not to answer it and just pretend I wasn't home. But the lights were all on, and if I didn't entertain him now, he would just come back later. I wished I hadn't just shed a few tears because my eyes were red and puffy, but he'd seen me cry enough times that it didn't really matter anymore.

I answered the door, my invisible armor protecting my body from his sword. I gave him a cold look and kept my hand on the door so he wouldn't come inside. Just like the last time I saw him, he looked forlorn. "I told you I—"

"I love you."

The words pierced the cold air like a bullet. It was quiet outside because it was snowing and everyone was staying indoors. I gripped the handle a little harder, shocked by what he'd said.

"I'm sorry I didn't say it before. But I'm saying it now. I'm sorry for the way I treated you. It was cruel, pathetic, and unforgivable. But I'm a better man now, even though I didn't see it for so long. I'm a better man, and I will be the man you want me to be. I love you, I trust you, and if you'll forgive me, I would like to start over…"

I listened to every word and memorized them, but still couldn't believe it. Paralyzed, I stood in front of the door and continued to block it, unsure what else to do.

Slate studied me closely, waiting for some response or reaction.

"I…I didn't expect you to say that."

"I didn't either…until Coen made me realize what I was doing."

"And what were you doing?" I whispered.

"I was behaving just like Simone, hurting you so you couldn't hurt me. I wanted to love you from the beginning, but I couldn't because I was too afraid. So I treated you like a transaction, a good I bought at the store. But it was all just to mask what I really felt. Someone hurt me, and I never got over that. So I turned into a different version of that...just to protect myself. I'm disgusted with myself, not just because of the way I treated you, but because of the way I allowed it to impact my entire life. I'm sorry for that...I really am." He didn't try to come inside as he bared his soul to me on the doorstep. Sincerity shone in his eyes, the kind of truth that burned all the way from his soul. "I'm not saying this just to get you back. This is the way I feel...the way I've always felt."

I'd stood at the kitchen counter just minutes ago, tears leaking down my face because we were never getting back together. Now he was on my doorstep, saying things I couldn't have even dreamed of.

"Cherry."

I lifted my gaze because my eyes had wandered to the ground in between us. My hand loosened on the doorknob because I suddenly felt lighter than air. All the sleepless nights were over. All the longing was in the past. "I...I didn't expect you to say all of that."

"I know. I should have said it a long time ago. I just hope it's not too late."

The man I loved was standing right before me, scared that I wouldn't take him back. It was ridiculous because he was all I ever wanted. I went out to a bar to meet someone else, but I had to force myself to do it. All I wanted was to go home to one man, to sleep in his bed every night and never look for someone new ever again. "Of course, it's not too late."

He crossed the threshold and slid his hands into my hair just the way he used to. His foot kicked the door shut behind him, and he kissed me under the antique chandelier. His fingers became reacquainted with my hair, and his lips softly treasured mine. It was the same kiss he'd been giving me for months, but this time, it was different.

This time, it meant something new.

He gave me purposeful kisses as he felt my mouth, as he

adored me with his sexy embrace. His hands trailed down and felt other parts of my body, from the skin over my collarbone to the curves of my hips. He enjoyed me like he'd never had the opportunity before, like he needed all of me right then to feel sane. It'd been an eternity since I'd been the recipient of that kiss—and it set me on fire.

He guided me into the living room as he pulled my top over my head. Clothes dropped to the floor, and we were naked in seconds because we were so anxious. His chiseled physique was searing hot to the touch, like he was a personal heater that could keep this entire place warm.

He guided me to the air mattress, and the second we were on the flimsy material, we rocked and shifted from our heavy weights. He was twice as heavy as I was, so he made the air mattress practically burst. It kept rubbing against the floor and making loud popping noises as we got into position.

It didn't deter him in the least. He got me in the position that he wanted, my legs pinned back and my body completely open to him. He moved on top of me and dominated me with his size, covering me completely and keeping me warm.

"I want to make love to you." His hand moved into the back of my hair, and he gripped me tightly. "For the first time." He slowly pressed his head inside me, found my moisture, and then slid completely inside.

"Slate…" I hadn't felt him between my legs in so long. It'd felt like months rather than weeks, and the last thing I wanted to do was go home with any other man. I only wanted this man inside me, this man who had all of me.

He looked me in the eye as he paused on top of me, his large dick stretching me wider than it ever had before. He throbbed inside me, like his cock was reunited with exactly where it wanted to be. His lips brushed mine, but he didn't kiss me. Instead, he teased me, his massive girth teasing me as well.

"Make love to me," I said against his mouth.

"I want to savor this." He placed a soft kiss on the corner of my mouth before he kissed my jawline. "Because I've never made love to a woman before—you're my first."

———

MY ALARM DISTURBED the silence of the living room. The faint sound of cars driving past the front of the house registered in my mind. In his penthouse, it was dead silent so I was used to the sound of nothing, but after a few days, I'd gotten used to the quiet sounds of life.

I grabbed my phone and silenced the alarm.

His naked body was wrapped around mine, his weight putting the maximum pressure on the air mattress before it popped. Any movement he made caused the air mattress to shriek in protest of his size. Without opening his eyes, he pulled me tighter against him. "Turn that shit off."

"It's off. But we still have to get up."

"We aren't going anywhere." He rolled me to my stomach then moved on top of me, his strong abs brushing against my backside. His hard dick rubbed between my ass cheeks as he pressed his face against the back of my head. His lips moved into my hair, and he inhaled deeply, like he wanted to treasure my smell.

"We both have work."

"The office doesn't need me. And you're calling in sick."

There was nothing I wanted more than to stay there with him, making love on that cheap air mattress all day. "I would, but I have a presentation this afternoon..."

He growled in my ear.

"I'm sorry."

He pressed on the top of his shaft and guided his head inside my slick entrance. "You'll have to make it up to me later."

"That sounds fair."

He sank inside me perfectly, gliding until he was balls deep. He used to struggle to get inside me, but now my pussy had been molded to his girth. I could take him just enough to make him fit, but I was still as tight as before. He bent his neck down so his lips could be near mine. "Cherry, you feel so good."

"You feel better."

He kissed the corner of my mouth as he started to rock, shifting the mattress with his movements. The momentum made me shift forward even farther, my body bouncing back and sliding onto his dick once more.

He took it nice and slow like I liked, enjoying my mouth just as his dick enjoyed my pussy. His lips felt mine with purpose, enjoying their fullness and softness. He breathed into me as he started to moan, as if he hadn't just had me twice the night before.

My orgasms happened faster than they had before, probably because the man I loved, loved me in return. It wasn't just sex anymore. It was my fantasy, exactly what I hoped I would find someday. I had a man who cared about me, who took care of me, and who loved me with everything that he had.

That was enough to make me explode.

My pussy tightened around him instinctively, gripping him with a powerful force. I felt the moisture pool around him and make him even slicker than he was before. His come was still inside me from the night before, and I felt his cock push it deeper inside me. "Slate...yes."

"This is your favorite position, isn't it?" he asked, breathing into my ear.

"Yes..." He was so deep at this angle, and I felt dominated completely. I'd never wanted to be dominated before I met him. I wanted Prince Charming, a chivalrous man who would open doors for me and wait until I was ready. Instead, I got a much darker, moodier man. But I wouldn't change anything.

His body stiffened noticeably, gave a small jerk, and then shuddered as he climaxed. He let his cock sit completely inside me as he finished, filling my cavity with another impressive load of come. He let out a small moan of pleasure, enjoying his orgasm as much as I enjoyed my own.

When he finished, he stayed deep inside me.

I wanted another round, but I was already going to be late to work as it was. "I have to go…"

He growled against my ear.

"But when I'm off work, I'm all yours."

"You're always mine—whether you're at work or not." He kissed my shoulder before he slowly pulled his softening dick out of me. He rolled over then got off the air mattress to grab his clothes.

I was excited to sleep in his bed again. That air mattress was starting to hurt my back. I got to my feet then picked up my clothes off the ground.

"I can take your stuff with me back to the penthouse." He pulled his long-sleeved shirt over his rock-hard body then grabbed his coat from the plastic chair.

"Why?"

He buttoned the coat all the way up to the top since it was snowing outside. "What do you mean why?"

"Why do you want to take all of my stuff?"

"Because you aren't living here anymore."

"I'm not?" I asked, unable to keep the surprise out of my voice. Just because we got back together didn't mean he wanted to live together. I figured nothing about that had changed.

"No. You're living with me. You think I'm going to let you stay here by yourself?"

"You were at one point…"

His eyes flinched at the insult. "I want you to live with me. I just assumed you knew that."

"You do?" I whispered. Knowing that he loved me and wanted me was enough. I didn't expect anything else.

"Yes. I want you in my bed every night. I haven't been able to sleep since you left...until last night. It doesn't feel right without you there. Even with Coen around, I feel so lonely. I've been drinking beer and eating chips nonstop."

"Whoa...you've been eating carbs?"

The corner of his mouth rose in a smile. "Yes."

"And I missed that?"

"We can have some beer and chips when you get home tonight."

"That sounds like a plan. But what about this place?"

He looked around the living room and shrugged. "It's yours. Do whatever you want with it."

"You bought it, Slate. It belongs to you."

"It's in your name."

I rolled my eyes. "If you're asking me to move in——"

"Telling you to move in."

"Then you should take it back. I never really lived in it anyway...just crashed on an air mattress in the middle of the living room." And spent my nights alone with a bottle of wine, with Coen for company sometimes. "I really don't want it and have no need for it."

"You don't want it for security? Just in case I act like an asshole again?"

I held his gaze as I rejected the suggestion. Slate had fucked up this relationship a lot, but I knew everything would be different from the second he arrived at my doorstep. He'd bared his heart to me, and it was completely sincere. "I don't need the security, Slate."

"I know you want marriage and kids, and I'd like to give that to you...someday. But not tomorrow."

"I never asked for tomorrow."

"If you kept this place, you would always have a backup if I screw things up again."

"You aren't going to screw things up, Slate."

"You think so?" He stepped closer to me, his eyes filled with fondness.

I rose onto my tiptoes so I could bring my face close to his. "I know so."

19

Slate

I HEADED TO THE OFFICE IN THE AFTERNOON BECAUSE I HAD a few things to take care. But I spent my morning putting Monroe's things back in the closet and taking a nap because I didn't sleep much the night before.

Because I was too busy fucking.

I walked into the building in my black suit and headed to Coen's office first since it was on the way. I talked to his assistants then let myself in to his office.

He was on the phone, his feet on the desk. "Yeah, let's do it. Pull the trigger." He hung up.

"Pull the trigger on what?"

"I'm taking golf lessons at the country club." He took his feet off the desk and relaxed in the leather chair. "I've always wanted to but never had the time. Simone said getting a membership was a waste of money. But that bitch is gone, so I can do what I want."

He should have been able to do what he wanted in the first place. "Good riddance."

"So...you didn't come home last night." He grinned. "What were you up to?"

I was surprised Monroe hadn't already told him since they were so close. "I slept at Monroe's."

His grin widened. "Yeah?"

"You seem awfully happy for wanting her for yourself."

He laughed like I'd made a joke. "You are such an idiot, Slate. I never wanted her."

"That's not what you said."

"I was just trying to get you jealous and worked up. I knew I was the last person you would want sniffing around Monroe, so I thought it would kick your ass into gear. Unfortunately, that didn't work."

"That was all a ploy?"

He nodded. "You really think I would backstab you like that?"

"Well…"

"Again?" he added. "No, I would never do that."

"And Monroe was aware of this?"

"She didn't like it, but she got on board. She was willing to do anything to make it work."

Now I felt like an idiot for getting so jealous. When I thought Coen wanted to fuck my girl, all I could see was red. I lost my goddamn mind because I was so insanely pissed. Now I was relieved it had never been true.

"I pressured her to go to the bar. And I pressured her to talk to that guy."

They manipulated me into behaving the way they wanted, but now that I had Monroe again, I didn't care that the pretenses had been false. She was mine, and that was all that mattered. "So you both played me?"

He shrugged. "Guess so. But we did it for your own good."

Because I had been sitting around and drinking my pain away. But the alcohol only made my pain even worse.

"But you're happy now, right?"

"Yes."

"Good. So, what now?"

"She's moving in with me."

"Awesome. Monroe was too much of a catch to let go. I wasn't going to let you make the biggest mistake of your life. I knew you were pissed at me at the time, but I really had your best interests at heart."

"Yeah...you did." My brother did whatever he could to get me back together with Monroe. He knew I cared about her even if I wouldn't admit it. He knew I wanted her for the rest of my life even though I was too scared to say it. "Thanks."

"Anytime. I'm just happy that you're happy. And I hope I find a woman like Monroe someday."

"You will, Coen."

He rose to his feet and came around the desk. "So, you tell her you love her?"

"Are we girls now?"

He smiled. "Did you?"

I nodded.

He clapped me on the shoulder. "Good. So, you love her, and she's moving in. My work is done. I can finally go back to my place now."

"Please do. I miss my privacy."

"No, you don't. You just want to fuck your girlfriend on the couch."

I glared at him.

"You know I meant that in a good way." He patted my shoulder. "Let's get some lunch to celebrate. I just need to grab something from the next room. I'll be right back."

"Alright." I watched him walk out before I looked out the window in front of me. He had the same view I did because his office was on the same side of the building. But he was on a lower floor, so the view wasn't as breathtaking. I looked out at the overcast sky and watched the snow fall down, feeling the peace inside my chest. Now I didn't feel pain. I only felt relief, optimism. I couldn't wait to go home and be with the woman I loved.

The woman I loved.

Like a weight had been lifted off my chest, I felt free. I'd been scared to feel anything for so long. I'd been afraid to trust anyone because everyone was so deceitful. But then I found an honest woman who liked me for me, and she would never betray me. It felt good to let the past stay in the past—where it belonged.

The door opened beside me.

I kept looking out the window. "Let's try that new—"

The cock of a gun filled the silent office. It was so distinct, I would recognize that noise anywhere. I wasn't a big fan of guns, but I knew how to use them and use them well. Without looking, I knew it was a pistol that was pointed right at me.

I turned to see a man in a black sweater, black pants, and a black mask pulled over his face.

Everything happened so quickly.

The man was in Coen's office, so that meant that gun was for him, not me. He didn't make any demands, didn't ask for money. He only had one mission—to kill Coen. Unfortunately, I looked just like him, and I was standing in his office. Anyone else would make the same mistake.

Better me than him.

I only had a second to react, and I had to make it count.

I knocked the gun away from me, but not before he pulled the trigger.

My body jerked as the bullet hit me right in the chest.

I didn't feel any pain, probably because my body was in survival mode.

The man fell to the left but quickly righted himself.

Coen ran back into the office when he heard the gunshot. "What the fuck?"

The man pointed the gun at Coen, realizing I wasn't the target. With a shaky hand, his finger went over the trigger.

Blood dripped down my clothes and fell to the ground, but that didn't stop me from protecting my brother. I launched my body at the gunman and knocked him to the ground as he squeezed the trigger. Bullets hit the ceiling and shattered the glass around us.

I got him to the floor, but instead of killing him, I grabbed the gun and slammed it into his skull. It took two hits before he finally passed out.

I took the bullets out of the gun and tossed them across the room.

"Slate!" Coen moved on top of me and ripped my shirt open. "Call 9-1-1!" he screamed to the girls at the front desk. "Shit, you're bleeding like crazy." He dropped his jacket then removed his own shirt so he could tie it around my body as a tourniquet. He pressed both of his hands against my chest and applied pressure to stop the bleeding. "Slate, stay with me."

I watched my brother work to save me, but my vision became blurry. I didn't feel any pain. All I felt was weakness, confusion. All I felt was my mind drifting away as my body began to fail me. It must have been the loss of blood that drove my weakness.

"Slate." He patted his hand against my cheek. "The paramedic is on the way. I need you to stay with me."

"I'm trying…" My eyes grew heavy.

"Slate, come on. Think of Monroe."

I tried to focus my thoughts, but I couldn't. I felt myself slip away.

"No! I'm not letting this piece of shit take you away from me!"

Then I was gone.

20

Monroe

I COULDN'T REMEMBER HOW I GOT FROM THE OFFICE TO the hospital. I couldn't remember if I ran, took a taxi, or even sprouted wings and flew there. The second he was mine again, he was taken from me—in the most horrific way imaginable.

By being shot.

In his own building.

By a fucking stranger.

I made it into the emergency room and then stumbled down the hallways as I looked for a familiar face. Everything happened so quickly, I hadn't had time to shed a single tear. My body went into defensive mode the second Coen told me the horrible news.

I still hadn't accepted it yet.

Coen came into my line of sight and grabbed me by both arms. "Hey, are you alright? You look like a ghost."

"Is he okay?" I blurted. "What's going on with him? Can I see him?" I refused to believe a single bullet would take down a strong man like Slate. His muscles were as thick as concrete. His bones were like steel. A single shot of metal couldn't take him down.

Coen's hair was a mess like he'd been fingering it constantly as he waited for news. "The bullet nicked an artery, so they took him to surgery. They're removing the bullet, repairing the artery, and giving him blood transfusions. He lost a lot of blood, so they're trying to stabilize him."

It was worse than I thought. "Is he going to make it...?"

"No one has given me an answer."

My knees suddenly felt weak and not because of the butterflies I usually felt when Slate was involved. I felt weak because I was broken. I hoped for good news, but all I received was horrific news instead. "He's gonna make it, right? He has to..."

"I hope so, Monroe. Slate is tough...toughest guy I know."

I nodded slightly, feeling the tears break the surface of my eyes and streak down my cheeks.

He pulled me into him and hugged me while nurses walked past us in the hallway. Family members held each other in the chairs against the wall. Doctors passed in their white coats. The speaker blared with an announcement every few minutes. I buried my face in his chest as I tried to block it out all out.

Coen held me like a brother, like a friend. He let me cry my heart out and stain his t-shirt with my tears. "We can't lose hope. Not yet."

"I know..."

"Slate will make it. I know he will." He pulled away and wiped my tears with the pads of his thumbs, his own eyes wet with tears that he wouldn't shed. "My mother has been so delirious, they had to give her a big dose of Xanax. She's a mess."

"Where is she now?"

"Asleep on one of the chairs. The surgery is going to be a few hours, so it was best to put her out of her misery."

"So, what do we know about the asshole that did this?"

His eyes suddenly moved to the floor, like he couldn't look me in the eye as he said the next part. He was ashamed, heartbroken, and crushed. "The man confessed to being hired by Simone. She wanted him to kill me so she could inherit everything I owned. Slate happened to be in my office alone when the man came in...mistook him for me."

I was going to strangle that bitch with my bare hands.

"That should be me in there."

"It should be no one in there, Coen. This isn't your fault."

"It is my fault. I should have listened to him about Simone... I shouldn't have gotten involved with her in the first place. This is karma, and I deserve every bit of it."

"That's not true, Coen. The only person who deserves the blame is Simone—because she was the psycho that decided to ruin everyone's lives. Don't you dare take the blame on your-self. Slate wouldn't want you to."

"I know he wouldn't...but if he dies—"

"Let's not even talk like that."

He nodded slightly. "You're right."

"What's going to happen to Simone?"

"They're searching for her. When they find her, they'll make an arrest. With a direct confession like that, a clear motivation, and the fact that she'd been missing for so long, it should be a slam dunk case. She'll be in prison for a long time."

"At least she'll get the punishment she deserves."

"Yeah...I just can't believe my ex-wife will be a criminal."

"Life is crazy sometimes..."

"I'll say."

I rubbed his arm to comfort him. "I guess all we can do now is wait...and pray."

21

Slate

MY EYES FLUTTERED OPEN, AND I SAW THE MONITOR beeping above me.

The doctor stood over me, his white coat in my line of sight. He flashed a light in my eyes and examined my face before he pulled away. "Mr. Remington, how are you feeling?"

I gathered I was in the hospital, but I had no idea how much time had passed. The last thing I remembered was being shot in my brother's office. "Alive, I think."

He chuckled. "You're definitely alive and in good shape. We repaired the artery, did a few blood transfusions, and got that chunk of metal out of your chest. You'll make a full recovery, but you'll need to rest for a while."

I'd forgotten that I'd been shot. The memory of that asshole with the gun came back to me. "Is my brother okay?"

"No one else was hurt. Just you, unfortunately."

I opened my eyes wider and looked around the room, but there were no visitors. "Can I see my family?"

"Yes, they're very eager to see you. I just wanted to check on you first. You'll be free to go in the morning."

"How much time has passed."

"Since you were shot…about thirty-six hours."

Thirty-six hours was a long time for my family to wait to see if I would be okay. My mother must have been a wreck. And Monroe…I didn't even want to think about her. "Send them in, please. All of them."

"Of course, Mr. Remington." The doctor walked out, and a few minutes later, my brother stepped inside. He was an unemotional guy, but he looked at me like he was going to break down in tears. He came to my bedside, grabbed my hand, and then rested his other arm on my shoulder. "How are you feeling?"

"Alive."

He smiled slightly. "I was scared for a second there."

"No reason to be. It would take more than a bullet to kill me."

"I know." He leaned down and kissed me on the forehead, something he'd never done before. "I love you, man."

"I love you too, brother." I gave him a gentle pat on the arm because I was still weak.

He pulled away so Mother could get to me.

She was a wreck.

"My baby." She leaned down and hugged me tightly, careful not to put pressure on my chest. Her tears dropped onto my neck, and she shivered as she held me. "I was so worried about my baby…"

"I'm alright." I rubbed her back gently. "The doctor said I'll make a full recovery. Everything is going to be okay."

She kept crying against me, because she needed the moment to know that I was really okay. That I was the same strong man I was just days ago. I might be weak in a bed right now, but that wouldn't last forever.

"I love you, honey." She pulled away and kissed me on the forehead.

"I love you too, Mother."

She squeezed both of my hands before she pulled away,

tears still streaming down her face. "I know Monroe is more anxious than all of us, so..." She stepped to the side and joined my brother.

Even with puffy eyes and tearstains on her cheeks, Monroe looked like the most beautiful woman in the world. She was exhausted, scared, and happy all at the same time. She came to my bedside, said nothing, and then rested her forehead against mine.

My hand moved into her hair, and I held her close, grateful I was alive so I could appreciate this moment. The right woman walked into my life a long time ago, but I was an idiot and didn't appreciate her. Now she was mine, and I would live long enough to enjoy her.

Neither one of us cared that other people witnessed our affection. My hand continued to stroke her hair, and I felt at peace in her presence, like she was the only person in the world who truly understood me. She completed in a way my own family didn't. She loved me unconditionally, accepted me for who I was. She loved me despite my flaws. She didn't love me because of my money. She loved me—for me. I opened my eyes and looked at her lips. "Marry me."

She inhaled a deep breath at the request, her eyes snapping open so she could look into mine. She pulled back slightly so she could get a better look at me, to make sure I was sincere and not just high on painkillers.

"I'm serious. I almost died. I could die tomorrow or the next day. I found the woman I love, and I want to be with her. So, will you marry me?"

Her eyes softened.

"I don't have a ring..."

"Yes, you do." My mother pulled her wedding ring off her left hand, the ring my father gave her thirty years ago. It was a white gold band with a single solitaire diamond in the center. "I want you to have it." With tears in her eyes for a new reason altogether, she placed the ring in my palm. "It would make your father and me very happy." She closed my fingers over the ring.

"Thanks, Mother." I turned back to Monroe, who was now sniffling as she tried to combat tears. I grabbed her left hand and held the ring close. "You better say yes. I'm putting this ring on your finger regardless."

She chuckled, but that also made her cry harder. "You know my answer is yes."

I slipped the ring onto her finger, and as if it was meant to be, it fit perfectly. "You're officially mine now. You'll have to put up with my bullshit, my stubbornness, and my carb-free lifestyle every single day."

"And I gladly will." She cupped my cheeks and leaned in to kiss me.

My arms wrapped around her, and I held her close, even if it caused me a bit of pain against my chest. It was worth it just to hold her, to know I had my whole life ahead of me. And I had the chance to correct all of my mistakes.

———

MOTHER WENT home to get some sleep, Monroe left to take a shower, so I lay in bed with Coen at my bedside.

"It's almost ten. You should go home."

"It's alright." He sat in a stiff chair against the wall and stared at the TV in the corner, which was on but muted.

"I'm just going to sleep."

"You should sleep."

"Coen, come on. I've got my nurse if I need anything."

"Drop it, alright?" he snapped. "I'm not going anywhere. Get over it." He pulled his gaze away from the TV and looked at me.

Since he was getting agitated, I let him be. "What do you know about the shooter?"

"How about we talk about that later?"

"Coen, it's not like you're going to give me a heart attack. I want to know who that asshole was."

He sighed with dread. "The police interrogated him. Turns out, Simone hired him to kill me."

It was so ridiculous that I couldn't believe it, but since it was Simone, I really could. That woman had been nothing but a nightmare since the moment I fucked her when I was fifteen. She'd been following me around like the plague ever since.

"The shooter thought you were me. That was why he shot you."

"I deduced that on my own. So, what about her?"

"The police found her hiding out somewhere in the Hamptons. She was staying with some rich boy toy. Now she's in jail without bail. The trial will be swift and easy. She'll probably get life without parole."

"Good." That was exactly what she deserved.

"I'm sorry, Slate. I should have listened to you…"

"Don't blame yourself, man. Simone is the psychopath here. She manipulates people like a profession. She's a leech that sucks people's blood and poisons them at the same time. Her beauty masks her ugliness."

"I still should have listened to you. And karma served me right."

"You didn't deserve this, Coen. No one deserves this."

He stared at his hands in his lap. "So, you're an engaged man now, huh?"

Asking Monroe to marry me was completely spontaneous. But when she walked into the room and lit up every single corner, I knew how much I wanted her. And in that moment, I knew I wanted her forever. All the fears I had were gone. That connection we had was special; it was real. I didn't want to live with her for a year before I finally committed. I just wanted to do it, regardless of how short our relationship had been. I wanted to be happy every day for the rest of my life—starting now. "I am."

He smiled. "I'm happy for you. And that was romantic as hell."

"Thanks…I didn't plan it at all."

"That's why it was romantic. And then when Mother gave you her ring…pretty epic."

Yes, my mother basically gave her approval of Monroe when she did that.

"I'm sorry it took getting shot to get you to commit, but at least it happened."

Getting shot certainly wasn't fun. "I'm glad all of this is over. I'm glad Simone is gone. I'm glad I've finally gotten over my fears. I'm glad you and I have a relationship again. It seemed like everything worked out in the end…"

"Yeah," my brother said with a nod. "But you know what the beautiful thing is? It's only the beginning."

Epilogue

SLATE

THE SUNLIGHT PIERCED THE WINDOW IN THE BEDROOM AND hit me right in the face. It was a spring day, the first sign of warmth after the long winter we'd had. The skin of my face started to feel warm, but I was too stubborn to open my eyes and get the day started.

"Can we do it now?" Charles's voice sounded from the outside of the bedroom door.

"Yeah," McKenzie said. "Daddy will like my toast."

"Daddy isn't awake yet," Monroe whispered.

"He's been sleeping all day," Charles argued. "Is Daddy a bear? Bears hibernate."

I couldn't stop the corner of my mouth from rising. My eyes stayed closed because I was so comfortable, but it was nice to hear my family talking right outside the door. Their hushed conversation filled me with more happiness than I'd ever known in my entire life. I thought my wedding day was the happiest day of my life, the turning point from when I changed from a bitter and angry man into a happy one. But making a family was what really made all the difference.

I finally opened my eyes and sat up in bed. I grabbed my

phone and set it down loudly then kicked the covers around so they would know I was awake.

Charles heard it first. "Mommy, I can hear him."

"The bear is awake," McKenzie whispered.

"Alright, let's go." Monroe opened the door and peeked inside first. "Morning."

"Morning." I sat up in bed, my eyes still heavy from the great night of sleep I'd had. My wife wore her plaid pajama bottoms and one of my t-shirts. With no makeup and just a smile on her face, she was a fantasy walking through the door.

Monroe carried a tray of breakfast and placed it over my lap. "The kids and I made you breakfast in bed."

Judging by the perfect way the scrambled eggs looked, Monroe had done that part. Everything else was a mess, like Charles and McKenzie had no idea what they were doing but insisted on helping. "Wow, it looks great."

"Happy birthday, Daddy!" Charles climbed onto the bed and jumped on my shoulders.

"Thanks, champ." I let him climb all over me like he was a spider monkey.

McKenzie was three years old, so climbing on the bed wasn't as easy for her. Monroe picked her up and placed her on my other side. "Happy birthday, Daddy." She kissed me on the cheek then helped herself to a piece of toast.

"Hey, I thought that was for me," I said with a laugh.

McKenzie kept eating.

Monroe sat at the edge of the bed and watched me with our two children, the light of happiness bright in her eyes. She'd always wanted a family, and she'd had to pressure me to do it at first, but once I caved, I'd never been happier. Now she got to see me love our kids, see me love them even more than she did. "Coen and Emily are coming over with the kids. We thought we would all go to the zoo."

"That sounds like a good day."

Charles grabbed the other piece of toast and started to eat it.

Monroe joined in by grabbing the fork and taking a bite of my eggs.

I'd learned that having a family was about sharing. There was no such thing as privacy, and as soon as something was out in the open, it belonged to everyone. I didn't even get birthday sex that morning like I used to before she became pregnant with Charles, but that was okay. A lot of things had changed—but in many good ways.

The four us devoured the contents on the plate until every single morsel was gone. Charles got the last piece of bacon.

"Thanks for breakfast in bed, guys. I appreciate it." I kissed each of them on the forehead before I set McKenzie on the ground.

"It's time to get dressed for the zoo," Monroe said. "Grab your shoes."

The kids left and went to their rooms.

Monroe lifted the tray and placed it at the side of the bed. "I know the zoo isn't at the top of your bucket list, but I thought it would be fun for all of us."

"It will be fun. You know the only thing I want for my birthday." Her dressed in slutty lingerie and on my bed, her hands tied to the headboard so I could enjoy her however I wanted. Now we always had to wait until the kids were asleep before we could do anything nasty.

"Yes, I do know. Which is why Coen and Emily have agreed to take the kids for the night."

My eyes narrowed on her face, and instantly, I forgot about the breakfast tray the kids had made for me. They were the lights of my life, the people I loved the most. Monroe used to be the most important thing in my life, and it was crazy how much that changed the second Charles was born. I loved my wife with all my heart, but my love for my children was much deeper. But I loved those intimate moments with

Monroe, moments that nothing to do with being a father to our kids. I loved when it was just the two of us, fucking like we had nothing else in the world to worry about. "Yeah?"

"Yes. That's my birthday present to you. Coen says he wants credit too."

"I don't care who takes credit. When is he taking them?"

"After dinner at six."

That meant I had all night with her—and all morning. "That's the best birthday gift ever."

She chuckled. "I thought you might like it. I also have another surprise for you…"

Please be lingerie.

She went to her dresser and pulled out a white one-piece with an open crotch. Lacy and thin, it was sexy as hell. With a deep cut in the front that would barely contain her tits, it was perfect. "Maybe you'll see me wear this later."

"And maybe I'll see it on the bedroom floor later."

"Maybe." She crawled up the bed until she straddled my hips and looked down into my face. "Can you wait that long?"

The idea of waiting all day felt like torture, but the wait would just make it even better. "You'll make it worth my while, Cherry." Every time I made love to her, I was turned on by the fact that I was the only man who had ever been inside her. She was pure, untouched, and so sexy. Every time felt like the first time.

"You know I will." She wrapped her arms around my neck and kissed me. "I love you."

"I love you too." I rubbed my nose against hers, wanting to treasure this quiet moment forever. But the thing about having young kids was the terrible chaos that existed at all times. They were only quiet when they were asleep, and if they were quiet when they weren't asleep, that wasn't a good sign.

Charles started yelling down the hall, and McKenzie cried a moment later.

I wanted to hold my wife like this a little longer, to have this connection stretch indefinitely. But I had to share my heart with two other people.

"It's just you and me tonight."

"Yes. But I prefer it when it's all four of us."

"You do?" She smiled as she cupped my cheek.

"I wish I had more time with you sometimes, not just the nighttime. But no, I wouldn't change anything. I never knew how much I wanted this until I had it. And now I wouldn't trade it for anything." I leaned in and kissed the corner of her mouth. "Our lives will pass so quickly now...because time flies when you're happy. And I'm very happy."

From Hartwick Publishing

You might also enjoy this book from New York Times Bestselling author, Penelope Sky.

Keep reading for a sneak peak at The Banker.

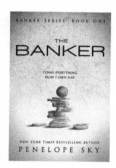

They've taken my father. They'll take me next unless I comply with their demands.

Taking down the most powerful man in Italy.

Cato Marino.

The man is accompanied by his security team everywhere he goes. His fortress in Tuscany is impenetrable. He's the most paranoid man in the country.

And there's no possibility I'll be able to take him down alone.

If I want to save my father, I only have one option.

To get into Cato's bed...and stay there.

———

The Banker - Chapter 1

SIENA

My grandmother left me a small house outside Florence. It was old, a living antique. The pipes were original, and I could hear the water running through the entire house when I flushed the toilet. There were cracks in the stone outside, and the glass in the windows was so aged that they were constantly blurry, regardless of how many times I cleaned them. It was a short distance from the city, so close that I never felt like I was really out in the middle of the Tuscan countryside, but it gave me the quiet and peace I craved. Every morning in spring and summer I could hear the birds chirping outside my window. It'd been a haven to me for a long time—since I'd turned my back on my family.

But right now, this house couldn't protect me.

I sprinted up the wooden staircase, the creaks screaming beneath my feet as I moved as quickly as my body could carry me. There was no point in being quiet—not when they knew I was here.

"Run, bitch." Damien led the chase, his two cronies behind him. "It's more fun this way." His sinister tone reached every end of the petite home, as if he were speaking over a sound system that amplified every single syllable.

"Shit." I made it upstairs and slid across the hardwood floor toward my mattress. Tucked in between the two pieces of the bedding was the revolver I kept for emergencies. I'd disowned my family years ago, so I'd thought I would never need it.

Guess I was wrong.

I turned off the safety and prepared to shoot Damien right between the eyes. I wasn't the kind of person who hesitated when they squeezed the trigger. It was either him or me.

It certainly wasn't going to be me.

Damien took his time moving up the stairs, his heavy footfalls beating like the sound of steady drums. "Sweetheart, I would check that gun if I were you." His deep voice carried down the hallway, his smile so audible I could actually see it behind my eyes.

My hands started to shake.

I opened the barrel and looked inside.

Empty.

"You've got to be kidding me…" They must have hit my house while I was at work, stripping away all my bullets so I would be unarmed when they came for me. It was smart on their part—because I was a good shot. "Fucking asshole."

His laugh drifted down the hall, the sound getting louder because he was so close. He seemed to move slower the closer he approached, as if he wanted to savor this for as long as he could. He cornered me like a rat—and he wanted me to squirm.

I was no rat—and I didn't squirm.

I opened my closet and pushed back all my shoe boxes until I found my sword—a samurai sword given to me as a gift from Kyoto. I removed the sheath and prepared the blade, ready to stab my attacker right through the neck as I'd been taught. I wasn't a master of the sword, but I certainly knew how to stab someone.

I pressed my back against the wall and waited for Damien to walk through the open doorway.

Damien cocked his gun before he moved inside, his gun held at shoulder height. "Sweetheart, you know I love it when you run—"

I slammed my blade down fast, aiming to sever his arm right at the elbow.

Damien must have been expecting me to hide there because he dodged out of the way. "Ooh...you look pissed."

I slashed my sword at him again.

He jumped out of the way and kept his gun aimed at my right shoulder. "And sexy." The corner of his mouth rose in a smile that looked more like a sneer. He was enjoying this way too much. His jet-black hair flopped down in front of his face and hid some of his left eye from view. He was the top dog in the organization—because he loved his job so much.

I stabbed my sword at his gut, wanting him to bleed out all over my floor.

He backed up toward my bed. "Sweetheart, I will shoot you."

"And I will stab you." I put all my strength into the move, preparing to drive my sword right through his gut and into the wall behind him.

He pulled the trigger.

I didn't feel the bullet enter my shoulder, just the jerk of my body at the momentum. My shoulder jutted back and my body shifted because the force was much stronger than my own velocity. Smoke burned from the tip of his gun. The smell was suffocating—along with that of my own blood. It was the first time I'd ever been shot, and the shock that washed over my body protected me from the pain.

I stayed on my two feet—refusing to fall.

I held his gaze, my eyes narrowing with a promise of death.

Damien dropped his smile, and against his will, he showed a slight look of respect. "Damn, you're stubborn."

"Damn, you're a bad shot." He'd hit me in the shoulder, missing the main arteries and organs.

"No. I hit my mark perfectly." He kept the gun trained on me, this time aiming it between my eyes. "Drop the sword. Or die." The barrel didn't shake as it stared me down. "What's it gonna be, sweetheart?"

I wanted nothing to do with this life. While I loved my father, I'd told him I wanted nothing to do with his business. By putting some distance between us, I'd thought I could have my own life, a reputation untarnished by the criminal underworld.

It looked like it had followed me anyway. "What do you want from me?"

"Drop the sword."

"What do you want from me?" I hissed. Blood was ruining my clothes and dripped down my arm. Dizziness settled in my brain. My strength was slowly starting to drift away, but I kept myself upright, like I had something to prove.

"What does it matter?" He tilted his head, his eyes narrowing in irritation.

"Because I need to know if it's worth dying for." I wasn't the kind of person who could be a willing prisoner. Instead of surrendering, I'd much rather die. Maybe it was my family bloodline or my Italian roots, but I was the most stubborn woman on the planet. I'd rather die for what I believed in than submit to anyone.

He shook his head slightly. "You've always been a crazy bitch."

"I take that as a compliment."

The corner of his mouth rose again. "We have your father. If you want to save him, drop the sword."

I continued to hold my pose, my heart beating harder in my chest. My father was being held captive, and if I died then and there, I wouldn't be able to help him. Damien had me cornered, and he knew it.

"Continue this suicide mission and die," he said simply. "Or come with us—and we'll work out a deal."

"Work out a deal?" I hissed. "You'll just take me and kill me too."

"Normally, yes. But I have another use for you. Drop the sword."

My hand wanted to keep gripping the handle, but there was doubt planted in my mind. Even if there was nothing I could do to save my father, letting myself die now wasn't an option. We fell apart a long time ago, but my loyalty had never waned.

I dropped the sword.

He grinned wide. "Good girl."

The Banker - Chapter 2
SIENA

THE MEN STOPPED THE BLEEDING THEN STITCHED UP BOTH
my entry and exit wounds, like this was an everyday occur-
rence. They didn't give me anything for the pain, and I was
too stubborn to ask. A thick piece of gauze was wrapped
around my shoulder, hidden underneath my t-shirt so I didn't
stick out like a sore thumb.

I was thrown in the back of the Escalade before they
escorted me into the center of Florence. It was five in the
evening, but the sun was still bright because it was summer-
time. We ventured down the narrow streets until we
approached an old building. With a tap of a button, a door to
the underground garage opened, and we descended.

It didn't bode well that they allowed me to see where we
were going.

I could have broken the window with my elbow and
jumped out of the car at any time. But if they really did have
my father, running wasn't an option. Regardless of our differ-
ences, we were family. He would lower his weapon for me in a
heartbeat...at least, I hoped he would.

We plummeted into the darkness of the underground
garage. Other expensive cars were parked in the spaces, all

SUVS and all black. After we parked, we got out of the car. The two sidekicks tried to handcuff me.

I kicked one in the shin. "Are you kidding me? I surrendered and I've been shot."

He clenched his jaw before he snatched my wrists again.

Like a horse, I slammed my leg back and bucked him.

Damien raised his hand. "Let her be. Nothing she can do anyway."

The guy finally let me go.

I kicked him again anyway, hitting him in the ankle.

He didn't hesitate before he backhanded me, hitting me hard across the cheek and making my body turn with the impact.

I moved with the momentum and almost tumbled to the ground, but I regained my balance before that humiliating event could occur. I righted myself again and glared at him, ignoring the tingling sensation in my cheek.

He pointed in front of him. "Walk, bitch."

"You know, I'm getting a little tired of this nickname." I stepped in front of him and followed Damien.

Damien opened the door and led the way. "I hope not. It fits you so well."

I was tempted to kick him in the back of the knee, but Damien would do something worse than slap me. I was already suffering from a gunshot wound, and I didn't want a stab wound to go with it.

He led me into the building and past a bar where the lackeys were enjoying their booze after a long day of criminal activity. Most of them looked me up and down like I was a plaything they would enjoy sometime that evening.

Not gonna happen.

I was led into a private room. With black walls and black-framed mirrors, it looked like a private room in a club. There was a bar in there too, but instead of having a bartender, there was just an older man in a black suit. He sat on one of the curved leather couches that faced a black coffee table. There were three glasses of scotch on the surface.

I was certain one of them was for me.

The goons shut the door behind us, leaving the three of us alone.

"She's damaged goods," Damien announced as he sauntered into the room. "But she didn't give me much of a choice. Pulled a samurai sword on me. She was pretty good at wielding it too." He approached his boss then turned to me. He snapped his fingers like a man calling to his dog.

I refused to cooperate. I probably would have sat of my own free will because booze was exactly what I needed to mask the pain. But comments like that weren't well received. My eyes narrowed, full of murder.

The man in the suit studied me with an unreadable expression. He had a gray beard that matched the hair on his head. His skin was tanned and tight, but he looked to be in his fifties. His age hadn't slowed down his muscularity, and he filled out the suit well. He still possessed enough strength to be a formidable opponent. "We treat our guests better than that." He rose to his feet then indicated the leather couch across from him. "I'm sure she's thirsty after the day she's had. Damien, get her a few painkillers to take with her scotch. No need for her to suffer."

If this guy were trying to kiss my ass, it wouldn't work. If he had a demon like Damien on his payroll, he definitely wasn't trustworthy. But the booze and pills were calling my name, so I took a seat. If they wanted to kill me, they would have done it already, so I knew their offering hadn't been poisoned.

I took the pills and washed them down with the scotch. I drank the entire glass, needing every drop to steady my nerves. Like my father, I didn't show fear in the face of danger, but a good glass of booze always made it a little easier. A drop dripped from the corner of my mouth, so I wiped it away with my forearm. "Let's skip the power plays and the bullshit. I need my father, and you need me. Elaborate." I rested my elbows on my knees as I stared at the gentleman sitting across from me. He seemed harmless, like a grandfather who only punished you when you really deserved it. But I wouldn't let the false kindness in his eyes overshadow who he really was.

He held his glass in the hand resting on his knee as he smiled at me. "Like father, like daughter."

"Not sure if that's a compliment or not." I'd inherited my father's hardness but not his lack of morality. I also had his eyes, but that was as far as our shared attributes went. Everything else I had I received from my mother, who'd been dead for many years.

"I'll let you decide." He took a drink before he set the glass on the table.

Damien sat beside him, his predatory eyes glued to my face. Lust and hostility shone in his gaze. He wanted to shoot me again just to get off on it. He was a demon without a leash. There was no telling what he might do.

They obviously needed me for something. Otherwise, I wouldn't be alive. If they wanted to torture my father and punish him, it would make sense to execute his only daughter. But I was still sitting there, the painkillers kicking in. "On with it." Perhaps I was bolder than usual because I knew I had some sort of power in this game.

"You know Damien well, obviously," he began. "But we haven't had the pleasure of meeting. I'm Micah."

"And you know who I am," I said, not bothering with an introduction. "Where is my father?"

"In the building." Micah wore a gold ring on his finger with a green emerald in the center. His hands showed his age, the veins mixing with the wrinkles. He must be a few years younger than my father. "The specifics don't matter."

"They matter if you want my cooperation." My father

taught me to always be strong, regardless of the opponent I faced. Earning your enemy's respect was the only saving grace you would ever receive. And if your fate was unavoidable, it was best to go out with honor. I was too proud to kneel for anyone—because that was how I was raised.

Damien gave a slow grin. "You're lucky you're alive right now."

I glanced to him. "As are you."

He widened his grin farther, hating me but wanting me at the same time. His green eyes were set in a handsome face, his masculine cheekbones complementing his full lips. He was a beautiful man, but he was tainted by such evil, his handsomeness got lost in translation.

Micah ignored his right-hand man. "If your father remains in my captivity, I will torture him and kill him."

I maintained the exact same expression, just as I would in a poker game. My brother was part of the family business, but he hadn't been mentioned once. He must have disappeared before they could get to him—and now they had no idea where he'd gone into hiding. He would never tell me, so it was pointless to ask. "I assumed. What do you want from me?" I didn't have special skills or any interaction with the family business, so I didn't have much to offer. Even my information was useless because I'd turned my back on the trade. That should be obvious to them—if they did their research.

"We'll make a trade with you," Micah offered. "One man for another."

I narrowed my eyes automatically, the fear involuntarily controlling my reactions. The only person they could possibly want was my brother—and that was a trade I refused to make. They could threaten to kill me again, and it still wouldn't make a difference. "You have a building full of capable men at your disposal. Why are you asking me?"

"This man is untouchable." Micah pulled out a folder

from the inside of his jacket and set it on the table between us.

I didn't open it. "If he's untouchable, I'm a terrible person to ask. I may be a good shot, but I'm no assassin." I couldn't pull off any kind of stunt. I lived a quiet life outside of Florence. I went to work every day at the gallery, spent time with my friends, had a few dates here and there, and then went home.

"We don't want you to kill him." Micah pushed the folder closer to me. "We need this man alive. Bring him to us, and your father goes free."

I couldn't allow myself to think about my father's condition. He was probably locked up in a room with no windows and barely a cot. Maybe he deserved it because of his business, but it broke my heart to imagine him that way. If there were anything I could do for him, I would. "As I've already said, I have no skills. I'm an art buyer."

Damien watched me with those malicious eyes. "Give yourself more credit, sweetheart."

I kept my gaze on Micah so I wouldn't rip out Damien's throat. "Who is this man?"

Micah grabbed his glass again, but instead of drinking from it, he held it in his palm. "Cato Marino."

That name meant nothing to me.

Micah must have recognized the blankness in my eyes because he elaborated. "He owns the biggest bank in the world. He hides money for the Chinese, has ties with the vaults in Switzerland, and half the debt of the United States can be attributed to him. There may be banks under different names, but they're all owned by the same man."

"Jesus…and you think I can touch this guy?" I laughed despite the seriousness of the situation because it was ridiculous. "He's like the richest dude in the universe. You think I can just walk up to him and ask him to come with me?"

"No." Damien watched me without blinking. "But you could get into his bed."

Now it became crystal clear. They wanted me to spread my legs and seduce this man. They wanted me to bed him like a whore. Once I gained his trust, I could trick him into being caught by the wrong hands. "I'm not in that line of business." I grabbed the bottle of scotch and refilled my glass.

"Then you better find another plan," Micah said. "It doesn't matter how you pull this off. As long as we get Cato Marino, your father walks free. It's that simple. Do nothing— and I will kill him." The gentlemanly attitude was long gone, and now his true colors rose to the surface. He squeezed his glass with his fingers. "Your father encroached on our territory and was stupid enough to cross the line one too many times. I was kind enough to give him a warning—but no more."

My father ran a cigar business, exporting them all across Europe. They were high quality, sometimes costing eighty euros just for a single one. But that wasn't how he made his money. His cigars were stuffed with drugs—the finest drugs in this hemisphere. He smuggled them where they needed to go under the clever disguise. The problem was, Micah was in the same line of work—and Italy just wasn't big enough for the both of them. I warned my father that his good luck would run out, that he would take a bigger bite than he could chew. When he didn't listen to me, I turned my back on my family —because I wanted a simple life.

"You're a clever woman, and I respect you." Micah had just threatened me, but now he'd flipped his attitude like it hadn't happened. "You didn't approve of what he was doing. You warned him this would happen. You left your family and started over. Unfortunately, the rest of your family didn't inherit the same intelligence."

"But I'm still here with you…so I can't be that smart." I should have left Italy. I should have moved to France or

London. Or better yet, I should have crossed the pond and started a new life in America.

Micah gave me a slight smile. "You can blame your father for that."

Yes, I could blame him for all of this. I wanted nothing to do with his criminal life, but I somehow had been dragged back into it. "What do you want with Cato Marino?" I didn't know anything about this guy, but I knew he wasn't innocent. If he were, Micah wouldn't be risking his organization to take down such a powerful man. There must be a good reason.

"Our business." Micah took a drink. "Not yours."

Why did I expect anything else? "And if I say no?" I had every right to walk away right now. I'd warned my father so many times. Even when my mother was murdered, he didn't stop. That was the last straw for me. He was blinded by greed and power. Fortune was more important than his family, more important than the woman who gave him his children. He got himself into this mess, and I should let him suffer for it.

Damien cocked his head slightly, as if that answer was the one he was hoping for. "Then you can join me in my bed." The threat was palpable, filling the air around us and permeating our skin. His lust matched his hostility, and there was no evidence of a bluff. "And when I'm done with you, I'll throw your dead body into your father's prison—naked and dripping with come from every hole."

Like bugs were crawling across my skin, I felt my body being twisted under invisible hands. My breathing picked up slightly, and my fingers flinched automatically, wishing I could grab a glass and smash it over Damien's head. But I already had a gunshot wound, and I wasn't craving another.

Even if Damien hadn't threatened me with that terrifying image, I knew my conscience wouldn't allow me to abandon my father. If he were anyone else, I would have kept fighting until the last drop of blood left my veins, but my loyalty wouldn't allow me to flinch. If I managed to pull this off, I would save my own life as well as my father's.

And the little girl inside me still wished we would have the fairy-tale ending I always wanted—a simple life together. Family dinners on Sunday. Putting up the Christmas tree while the frost pressed against the windows. Drinking wine at our favorite vineyard just when the harvest finished. I'd felt alone my entire life—even when my family was just a few miles away. "If I bring Cato to you, you release both my father and me?"

Micah nodded. "As long as your father shuts down his business."

My father loved that business more than me, but perhaps being locked up for god knows how long would change his mind. "Fine. But I'm not sleeping with him." I would do anything to save my family, but opening my legs wasn't an avenue I would take. There must be some other way to make it happen.

"It doesn't matter to me how you do it," Micah said. "Just get the job done. But if you fail, there is no deal. Until Cato Marino is in my captivity, your father will remain here. And if you can't deliver what you promised, I'll be forced to kill your father. So, if I were you...I wouldn't take your time."

Damien smiled at me. "But after I capture you again...I'll definitely take my time."

The Banker - Chapter 3

SIENA

THIS WAS WHAT I'D GATHERED ABOUT CATO MARINO.

He was stupid rich. Multibillionaire.

He was self-made. I couldn't wrap my mind around the achievements of this single man in his single lifetime.

He was young. He just turned thirty in March.

How did someone so young accomplish so much?

And the most surprising revelation of all…he was hot.

Inexplicably gorgeous. So beautiful it was unreal. Over six foot of steel—and probably all steel in his pants too. Every picture I saw of him showed off his caveman shoulders, his muscled arms, and tight waist. Whether he was in jeans or a suit, the hardness of his body couldn't be denied. Sexy from head to toe, he was model material, not just banker material.

I hadn't planned on seducing him to accomplish my goal, but now I realized that plan wouldn't have worked anyway. A hot billionaire like him was already getting too much ass to handle. He could have any woman he wanted, so there was no way I could impress him. He might glance at me, think I was pretty. But an instant later, he would already be thinking about something else.

I did as much research as I could, and it was safe to

conclude this man was impenetrable. Every photograph I could find of him showed his security team in the background. The only public appearances he made were for work. His personal life wasn't disclosed. There wasn't even a picture of him going to the grocery store to pick up some orange juice.

No wonder why Micah put this on my shoulders.

There were a few places Cato frequented in Florence, so I decided to get a view of him in person. Perhaps if I studied my prey, I'd gain a better understanding of how I was going to pull this off. Marching up to him with a gun wouldn't accomplish anything. One of his men would take me out in a second. I probably couldn't even walk up to him at all, not without being intercepted by one of his bodyguards.

I didn't have a lot of time to waste, but I had to take this slowly if I were going to accomplish anything.

I went to one of his favorite clubs in Florence. I didn't have a clue if or when he would show his face, so I made an appearance three nights in a row, wearing a different dress and heels each time. The bartender thought I was a lonely alcoholic who had quickly become a regular.

On the third night, I sat alone at a table when I finally got some luck. My hands were wrapped around my glass of scotch as my eyes watched the commotion at the doorway. Bouncers moved out of the way so Cato could lead the pack. With three other good-looking men in suits, they entered the bar, all heads turning their way like they were beautiful women in heels. Women weren't the only ones looking, but men too, probably envious of a man who was so rich and handsome he could have any woman he wanted—at any time.

A special seating area was cleared out just for them, and before their muscular asses pressed against the leather seats, a sexy waitress in a dress that hardly covered anything appeared out of nowhere to wait on them.

I focused on Cato and ignored his three friends. Even in the darkness of the club, he looked exactly the same as he did in his photographs. Rugged, handsome, and confident. He wore a gray V-neck that highlighted his muscular arms and chest. His shoulders were broader in person than they were in the pictures. With blue eyes and brown hair, he was a very pretty man. His tanned skin implied he loved the outdoors, even though I'd never seen a single photograph of him hiking or yachting.

I continued to enjoy my scotch as I stared from my chair, trying to glean as much information as I could. The three men with him seemed to be friends, not security detail. The men in charge of keeping him safe stayed near the entrance, their eyes scanning the bar and everyone near it. Hopefully, they didn't find me suspicious, just a woman who was debating making a move.

Just as the waitress returned with their drinks, a group of confident women joined them. All pretty and dressed for the occasion, they flashed their smiles and their long legs, knowing exactly who Cato was.

I assumed a handsome guy like him was a playboy, but I wasn't prepared for how extreme of a playboy he was.

He grabbed the woman closest to him by the wrist and gently tugged her toward him. His hands guided her hips over his thighs until she straddled his lap. Then he gripped her lower back and pulled her in for a kiss, her dress riding up and showing her black thong to everyone.

The other guys didn't seem the least bit surprised.

The bar staff didn't rush over and tell her to stick to the dress code.

With my jaw hanging open, I watched Cato make out with a complete stranger. Like he could do whatever he wanted, he took control without asking permission. His hand dug into her hair, and he kissed her with his full lips, treating her like he adored her rather than had no idea who she was.

His fingers tucked her hair behind her ear then he gripped her ass.

Even though he was a total pig, it was still pretty hot. He certainly knew how to use that rugged mouth of his.

He ended the kiss then gently guided her into the seat beside him. His arm rested over the back of the couch, and he turned to talk to her, perhaps to actually ask for her name, but another woman straddled his hips and stole his attention.

Then he made out with her next.

"Jesus..." I took a long drink of my scotch.

She kissed him harder than the previous woman, her hands scratching his chest as she ground against his erection in his slacks. She showed him her best moves, doing her damnedest to erase the woman who had just pulled the same stunt.

The kiss lasted a while before he directed her into the space on the other side of him. Both of his arms now rested on the leather of the back of the couch as he claimed both women for the night, one under each arm.

"Wow...what a pig."

The other guys found their women, and then they spent the night drinking and talking.

I'd had my fair share of playboys, but nothing of that caliber. That man didn't even need to hunt for pussy because it hunted for him. All he had to do was wait thirty seconds, and a beautiful woman would appear to replace the previous one. When the night was over, he would probably take both women back to his place with the intention of bedding them both. They probably hoped they might catch his attention if they were adventurous enough, but like all the others, they would be gone by morning.

And he would forget their faces forever.

Just when I finished my scotch, another woman appeared. She straddled his lap, and another make-out session commenced.

I'd been sitting there all night without attracting an admirer, while Cato was getting more pussy than he could handle. "Fuck...I need another drink."

———

I HAD a few friends in high places, so I used that to my advantage to get an audience with the right man.

A hitman.

He specialized in killing high-profile targets and making it look like accidents. He'd retired a few years ago, but he'd had an illustrious career that garnered him a great deal of respect. Bosco Roth was a good friend of my brother's, so I called him and asked for an introduction to this famous killer.

Now I sat on the bench at the bus stop in the middle of the night. It was two in the morning, and everyone was at home. The only company I had was a bum sleeping across the street in the alleyway. The sun had been gone for hours, but the humidity still hovered over me in the darkness. I was in jeans and a t-shirt, but even that was too warm to wear.

Heavy footsteps sounded to my left, and that's when I turned to see the huge man covered in sleeves of tattoos. He was terrifying in appearance, especially when he clenched his jaw like that. He didn't look the least bit pleased to see me, like this favor he was doing for Bosco was nothing but a pain in the ass.

I rose to my feet and stood under the lamplight. Like always, I didn't show fear, even though this man was much more terrifying than Damien had ever been. "Bones?"

He stopped in front of me, keeping several feet in between us. We were visible under the lamplight, but he didn't seem to care if we were seen. He was in a black t-shirt and black jeans, matching the ink that covered his arms and disappeared under the collar of his shirt. "I'm only here because Bosco is a friend of mine. I'm not in the game anymore, and there's nothing you can offer me to change my mind. If we're done here, I have somewhere to be." He spat everything out as quickly as he could, like just one more second of this meeting was too much for him.

When I was part of my family, I was used to luxury. We were a wealthy family, so I always had everything that I needed. Perhaps if I had stayed, that would still be the case, and I would have a lot more money to offer him. Unfortunately, all I had was the deed to my house, some jewelry my father bought me, and my car. "There's a million euros for you if you can help me." To me, that was a fortune.

But based on the coldness of his face, that was just a few pennies. "I said there's nothing you can offer me. I meant it." He slid his hands into his front pockets, and that's when I noticed the black ring tattooed on his ring finger.

"I don't want to kill this guy. I just need to get him from Point A to Point B." Now that I'd observed Cato with my own eyes, I realized how difficult this mission would be. He was impossible to access because he was never alone, and if he was alone, he probably had a woman's tongue down his throat. This was completely out of my league. "It's a simple mission."

"Then why do you need me?"

"This isn't really my forte…"

He continued to look bored.

"Look, I'm mixed up in some serious shit, and I need help."

Bones still look irritated, like every moment he wasted was precious. "I have a guy who can help you. But a million euro isn't going to cut it."

"Then how much?" Maybe I could scrounge up some more money somehow.

"Depends on the target. Who is it?"

I glanced around us to make sure we were alone. "Cato Marino."

Recognition immediately flashed in his gaze. "No one is gonna take the hit for less than a hundred million."

My eyes snapped open. "You can't be serious."

"He's a high-profile target. I'm not even sure it can be done. A hundred million is a conservative guess."

"I don't have that kind of money…"

"Then you don't have Cato." He took a step back like he was going to leave the scene. "I've got a wife and kid at home. I shouldn't have come in the first place."

"Wait, please."

He stopped and burned his ice-cold gaze into mine. "I just told you I can't help you. You're on your own, woman."

"Could you at least give me some advice?" I tried not to beg, but my voice slowly rose. If no one would help me, my odds of completing this mission were even more unlikely. Killing Cato would be a much easier task than delivering him to Micah. At least then I could hide on top of a roof and aim my weapon. "How would you capture Cato and hand him over?"

"Cato Marino is a powerful man. He's got security on him at all times."

"Hence, why I'm asking for advice." Maybe I shouldn't be a smartass right now, but I was losing my focus.

He narrowed his eyes. "You don't stand a chance. If you have no men and no money, capturing someone like him isn't possible. You only have one option, and even then, it probably won't work."

"What?" I asked, crossing my arms over my chest.

He stared at me for a few seconds, his eyes steady and wide. He didn't blink often, adding to his aura of constant hostility. "Fuck him. Fuck him hard."

THERE WAS a coffee shop across the street from one of

Cato's banks, and he'd been seen grabbing a cup of afternoon coffee there once in a while. He had been dressed in his suit and tie, and it seemed like he'd spent all morning talking about money until his brain was fried.

I sat at one of the tables outside with a latte and a book, hoping he would stop by sometime that week. A few days passed and he didn't make an appearance, and I was almost done with my book and would soon have to replace it. Thankfully, the gallery had been slow for the past two weeks, so my boss didn't need me as often as usual.

I could keep stalking my target.

Finally, Cato Marino showed up. It was two in the afternoon when he crossed the street and stepped inside the bakery.

I could watch him through the windows. He was in a gray suit and black tie. His trousers hugged his rock-hard ass, and he held himself with perfect posture. He stood in line and waited to order as he casually glanced at his expensive watch. Then he rubbed his fingers across the shadowy beard that started to pop up along his chiseled jaw.

I wondered if he'd gone home with all three of those women from the bar.

Wouldn't be surprised.

He moved up to the front of the line and gave his order. He dropped a hundred euro into the tip jar when no one was looking then stepped away to wait for his coffee to be prepared.

So the guy was generous.

I didn't know what these stalking sessions would accomplish. It didn't seem like I was gleaning any helpful knowledge in the process. So far, all I'd uncovered was that he was getting laid constantly and he looked damn good in a suit. He was also a generous tipper. But none of those things would help me get him into Micah's hands.

And regardless of how hot he was, I was not screwing him.

I'd have to find another way.

The barista handed him his coffee, and he took a sip before he walked out and crossed the street. He didn't look at me once because he didn't notice me in the center of filled tables. That worked out in my favor, because if he did notice me, I wouldn't be able to follow him anymore.

I watched him as he opened the door and stepped inside the bank, over six feet of muscle and pure masculinity. The suit fit him so well, clearly designed just for him, and he moved like a god rather than a human. The door shut behind him, and he was gone from my sight.

How was I going to do this?

————

I PULLED up to Barsetti Vineyards and left my car in the gravel parking lot. The sun was high in the sky, and out in the middle of Tuscany, there were iconic views of the land that made it so famous. The smell of olive trees was in the air, along with the succulent scent of grapes in the vineyard.

I walked onto the property then made my way into the main building. A friend of my father's ran the vineyard, and from what I could recall, he wasn't just a winemaker. His hands were just as dirty as my father's.

I checked in with his assistant before I stepped inside.

The last time I saw Crow Barsetti, I was just a child. His features weren't easy to remember because I was just too young, but I did remember his eyes. They were unique with their green and hazel color. Now decades had passed, and he was a different man from the one I'd met all those years ago —but his eyes were still the same.

He rose from behind his desk and joined me near the

door, examining me like he was trying to place me in his mind. "Siena Russo…are you Stefan's daughter?"

He had a good memory. "I'm glad you remember me."

"Vaguely," he said simply. "How can I help you, Siena? Your father well?"

"Uh…not really." I crossed my arms over my chest and hoped this man would risk everything to help me. It didn't make sense why he would, but I had to try. Maybe he would take pity on me.

"What is it?" Tall and strong, he was a man who had aged well. Spending his days working at a winery had obviously kept him in shape. There were pictures scattered across his desk, probably pictures of his family.

"My father has been captured by Micah and his men. My brother is missing, and I'm not sure what's going on with the business."

He sighed quietly. "I'm sorry to hear that, Siena." He seemed sincere.

"Micah made a deal with me. If I bring him a man he wants, he'll let my father go. If I don't…he'll kill me and my father." I left out the rape part. That was a subject no one ever wanted to discuss.

"Who's the man?"

"Cato Marino."

Crow sighed as he rubbed the back of his neck. "So he gives you a mission you have no chance of completing…"

"It seems that way."

"I'm sorry, Siena. I warned your father he should walk away from the business. A criminal life will only last so long… before that luck runs out. I stopped my weapons business when I married my wife. We both wanted a simple life."

"Good for you. I wish my father had done the same." Perhaps my mother would still be alive right now if he had.

He gave me a look full of pity. "I know you're going to ask for my help. But before you do, I have to tell you about my family. My brother and I have been running this winery for thirty years. Now I'm grooming my son-in-law to take it over. I have two grandsons. Reid is two and Crow Jr. is one."

I smiled. "He was named after you."

"Yes." His happiness didn't mirror mine. "I've fought many wars over my lifetime. I can't do it anymore. I'm very sorry, Siena. Truly. But I can't put my family in jeopardy, not when we finally have the peace we worked so hard for."

How could I argue with a man who just wanted to protect his family? He'd made the right decision when my father didn't. He'd walked away from his business and criminal ties to protect his family. He wasn't greedy and selfish like my father. He'd made the right call. "I understand." Crow Barsetti deserved the peace he'd fought for—and I would never take that away from him. "You're right."

He tilted his head slightly, his eyes full of pity. "Want my advice?"

"Please." I lifted my eyes to meet his.

"Run."

My heart started to palpitate.

"Your father wouldn't want you to risk your life for his. He wouldn't want you to attempt this mission and get killed. And if you fail, Micah will just hunt you down. Take whatever money you have left and run."

It was good advice, the same advice I would give to anyone else.

"Stefan had his chance to choose a peaceful life. He didn't take it. You shouldn't be punished for that, Siena."

He was absolutely right. I shouldn't be punished for my father's stupidity. "I agree with you. But my loyalty won't allow me to give up. His blood is my blood. I know if our places were switched, he wouldn't give up."

"That's different. He's your father. That's his burden—not yours. And as a father and a grandfather, I can promise you he would want you to run. He would want you to leave him to

die. If my daughter were in that position...I would want her
to run as hard as she could. My memory would live on with
her anyway."

It was a sweet thing to say, especially since it was so
sincere. "I still can't do it." I couldn't let my father rot in that
prison until they tortured him to death. "I would never be
happy anyway. I would constantly wonder if he'd been killed
yet. And if he had been killed, the guilt would haunt me
forever. He doesn't deserve my loyalty...but he has it
anyway."

AFTER I FINISHED work at the gallery, I walked a few blocks
until I reached the café Cato liked to frequent. This time, I
didn't stop by in the hope of seeing him. After the long day
I'd had, I wanted an iced coffee and a muffin to rip apart with
my fingertips.

Most people hated the brutal summers here in Florence,
but I didn't mind them at all. I'd grown up in this treacherous
heat, and I couldn't imagine my life without that experience.
So I took my coffee and muffin and sat outside. I had a client
who'd recruited me to decorate his summer home in Tuscany,
and now I was studying images of his living room and dining
room to determine the size and color of the frames as well as
the artwork that would complement each one. That was my
job—finding artwork for rich people. Sometimes people just
wanted cheap stuff to cover the walls, but occasionally, my
clients had more refined taste and preferred masterpieces by
local artists. Those always took longer to locate, but since I
charged by the hour, that worked out in my favor.

The chair across from me shifted, and then a heavy body
filled its vacancy.

When my eyes flicked upward, they landed on the man I'd
been hunting. With blue eyes that matched the summer sky

and a hard jaw that looked like it'd been carved with a knife, the beautiful man I'd been watching from afar sat in front of me.

He didn't greet me with that handsome smile I'd seen him flash to his women. Instead, his eyes were hostile and his lips were slightly pressed in amusement. He wasn't wearing a suit and tie like he usually did when he frequented this spot. Today, he was dressed in jeans and an olive green t-shirt, a V in the front so his chest muscles were unmistakable. At this close distance, I could clearly see the tight cords in his neck, the obvious tension of the muscles of his physique. His sunglasses hung from the vee in his shirt, and he rested his forearms on the armrests of the chair. They were flanked with the same veins that matched his neck, and he was the tightest and fittest man I'd seen. It seemed like he only worked out and ate protein. No wonder he could get three different women in a row to make out with him without even making an introduction.

He'd caught me off guard and he knew it, judging by the hint of arrogance in his eyes, but I refused to acknowledge it. My table was scattered with images of a living room and I was looking up artwork online, so it was clear I was actually working on something. I never allowed fear to enter my expression, so I remained as calm as ever. "Hello." That was the only response I would give him. Saying the least amount possible was the smartest thing to do in this situation. Maybe he'd figured out I'd been following him. Or maybe he was making a pass at me. There was no real way to know until he stated his intentions.

"My stalkers aren't usually young and beautiful women. This is a nice surprise." He sat forward and moved his fore-arms to the top of the table. His hands rested on my paper-work, but he didn't look down to examine my project. His eyes were glued to me and focused, like there was nothing else more important in the world than watching me. He didn't blink as he took me in, and it seemed like I was sitting across from him in a business meeting. I wouldn't be able to leave until I gave him what he wanted.

I kept my eyes on him as I shut my laptop. "Thank you. But I'm not a stalker."

His eyes narrowed slightly as he examined me. "Don't insult me. There's nothing that goes on around me that I don't notice." His voice complemented his appearance perfectly. It was deep and sharp, just like the edge of a knife.

Even though his assumption was totally accurate, I didn't like his arrogance. He was the conceited playboy I'd assumed he was. The whole world revolved around him—and him alone. Maybe I was just jealous that he could have hot sex every night of his life when I hadn't gotten action in over a month. Or maybe I hated men who thought they were better than everyone else. I used to be rich once upon a time. I knew how rich people thought—that they were above everyone. "Maybe if you weren't so cocky, you would realize it's just a coincidence. Not everyone wants your balls."

The corner of his mouth ticked slightly, like he wanted to smile but stopped himself from doing it. "If you don't want my balls, then why are you following me?" Within the short time he sat there with me, he'd drawn attention from the other tables. Women turned around to look at him, aware that the sexiest bachelor in Italy had spotted a random woman he liked.

What a wrong assumption that was. "Coincidence."

"Really?" He cocked his head slightly, his blue eyes taking me in aggressively. His wide shoulders looked broad in the cotton on his shirt, and the veins on his forearms moved all the way up to his biceps. "If you don't want my balls and this really is a coincidence, then I should never see you again." He rose to his feet and pushed the chair back at the same time. He walked off, turning his back on me and walking down the sidewalk. His ass looked snug in his jeans, and all the women in my vicinity noticed the exact same thing.

There was no mistaking the subtle threat in his tone. He let me off the hook because his formidable power was enough to chase anyone away. Unless I acted like I wanted to fuck him, he wanted nothing to do with me. If I had an ulterior motive, then I should stay the hell away from him.

But there was a problem with that.

I couldn't stay away—not if I wanted my father to live.

Order Now